Found Money

Found Money

By Mark T. Sneed

ISBN: 9781736669846

DEDICATION

To my mother, family and friends who continue to inspire, encourage, and challenge me to be a better person.

THANK YOU

To all the unsung dreamers, visionaries, believers, questioners, who possess the faith and belief in their convictions despite what others try to say or attempt to shout down what is impossible. Thank you for attempting to prove your beliefs, dreams, and ideas not to spite but to enlighten those of what a unique perspective and trust can manifest in the scope of what is possible.

Found Money

Found Money
By Mark T. Sneed

Table of contents

Chapter 1.
Ten o'clockish PM

Arriving at the warehouse on Fenkell Street the two boys had been searched for weapons and relieved of their backpacks, just long enough to make sure there were no weapons in them. The two were herded from the entrance to the first layer of security and threatened by a thug wearing an eye patch, like a pirate.

Once past the pretend pirate they were asked by several other thugs who they were looking for. They were searched again before meeting the man who was going to introduce them to Happy Hammond. The last man before Happy Hammond had a brown and oval shaped face, brown eyes, and thick lips. He was the only thug in the warehouse with a Drake heart cut into the front of his head. He was not skinny but not powerfully built either.

Happy Hammond looked a little like a black Pillsbury doughboy. He was nothing like Mase imagined. Mase knew he was supposed to be a drug kingpin running everything from Eight Mile to Oakman Boulevard and an unapologetic criminal and cutthroat, but the guy who was sitting on the third floor of the red brick warehouse didn't give that impression. He was a round bellied black man with a tiny smile on his round dark face. Hammond's smiling made Mase smile. It didn't matter that Happy Hammond was considered one of the most dangerous drug dealers in Detroit and linked to a dozen killings. His easy smile seemed infectious. Happy Hammond was maybe thirty and dressed in a black collared shirt, opened at the throat to show off the thick gold chain around his neck and the diamond encrusted B dangling from it. He was the uncontested leader of the Brethren.

His office was just a big wooden desk where Happy was sitting looking at a computer screen. On one side of the office space was a couple of old pinball machines, a big screen monitor and four gamers' chairs. There was a couch on the opposite side of the room up against the wall and nothing else. Two men were sitting on either side of the door when Mase and Book were brought into see Happy. They were strapped and seemed ready for anything.

"They had these on them when they walked in," the average thug said, lifting their backpacks, and looking at Hammond and then back at the boys. He was unusual because he wasn't dressed in a hoody or baggy jeans, instead he was wearing a Tigers car coat, collared shirt, dark pants, and dress shoes. Next to him was a Drake wannabe with a heart shaved into his hairline. He had a long stubble beard. The Drake impersonator was dressed in a black hoody with an embroidered B over his heart. On the back of the hoody was the detailed embroidered B of the Brethren.

"This from Chocolate?" Happy asked.

Mase and Book nodded their heads. Happy walked from behind his desk and approached the Drake wannabe with that easy smile. He looked at the boys and laughed, silently. He looked to the nameless man and grinned again.

"Rocko? You and Earl check the package," Happy said, looking at Drake's imitation and one of the thugs with them. He looked again at Mase and Book.

"Have them wait," Happy Hammond said and walked away from Mase and Book.

The two boys were walked out of the office and Drake and another thug unzipped the backpacks as Mase and Book were taken to the second floor.

The two boys were directed to a small room. The room had a few chairs and a broken desk. They were told to wait and guarded by four thugs. The four thugs all were armed and looked more than willing to murk either boy. After what seemed forever Rocko, the average thug, appeared and took the boys back up to the third floor of the warehouse and Happy Hammond.

"Tell Chocolate that we good for now," Happy said.

Mase nodded. He and Book looked at the round face and the friendly smile of Happy Hammond and prepared to leave. Hammond cleared his throat and Drake lifted two backpacks for the boys.

"Take this back to Chocolate," Happy said. "Tell him, we good, but we ain't square."

Mase and Book held onto the backpacks but did not move.

"Scoot," the powerful black man sitting behind his desk on the third floor of a warehouse, miles from downtown, said. He spoke and instantly bored with the two boys, focused on something else.

Mase and Book slipped on the backpacks and them and three men headed for the exit of the lush office of Happy Hammond. The three men, hooded sweatshirts, baggy jeans, and Timberlands stalked out of the office. One of them had French braids. One was bald with a hand tattoo and a tattoo with a name on his neck. The third one, Rocko, led.

Once out of the office another thug fell in step with the others. He had the biggest arms Mase and Book had ever seen. Around his thick neck was a thick gold chain which had a gold and diamond encrusted B hanging from it.

Outside of the warehouse the rain began to fall. The glass was splattered with a sprinkling of rainwater and then it let up. Mase watched the rain spitting against the windows and intensify for about ten minutes straight before letting up and becoming a drizzle. It was as if someone was turning on and off a sprinkler outside to wash the windows, Mase thought absently as the rain stopped a few minutes later.

With their backpacks on the two runners were led to the second floor. The group continued across the deserted second floor. Mase and Book noticed they were heading to the first floor of the three-story red brick warehouse. The two looked at each other nervously when they reached the second floor, guarded by the four, armed and tattooed, men.

"Lil nig, once I drop you off at the exit all yo' privileges are revoked," Rocko said as they descended the stairs to the first floor.

Book, with the short haircut and diamond in his earlobe, was wearing a black hooded sweatshirt, baggy jeans, and blue basketball sneakers. He had a waterproof white backpack on.

Mase, with a lightning bolt etched into the side of his tight fade had a hooded black sweatshirt, blue jeans, and basketball sneakers on his feet. On his wrist was a knock off Rolex. Around his neck hung a thick gold chain and a golden letter H. His backpack was green.

Mase, the older of the two, looked at Book who was lost looking at all the intricacies of the warehouse. He leaned over to Book and elbowed him. Book looked at Mase.

"As soon as we see air, we're ghost," Mase said to his play cousin.

Rocko walked on ahead of the two boys. On the first floor the pair walked through ten or twelve scowling faces who watched them like they were fresh meat. The warehouse, the two knew, sat on the eastern edge of Brethren territory.

Rocko stopped and one of the thugs in the warehouse pulled up one of the three rollup gates in the rear of the warehouse. The gate, once opened, was guarded by two Brethren. If it hadn't been for the four dim hanging lights which traced the fine spray floating in the dark that night in the courtyard, which was overlooking the loading dock Mase and Book would not have known, they were at an exit.

They were in the bottom of a block C-shaped warehouse. The loading dock rested six feet above the ground and opened out onto the dim interior courtyard which climbed to the streets on the westside of the warehouse.

"Run," Mase said to Book and with the order the pair jumped from the loading dock and landing ran from the Brethren's spot and into the dark and drizzling night. They splashed into the depressions which would become puddles after a steady rain.

"Don't get too wet," someone said from the warehouse.

Behind them they heard laughter. Mase ran to the left.

"Look both ways before you cross those streets," someone else said from behind with a laugh.

The two ran across the dark courtyard and up the short ramp to the street. Mase turned left, and Book followed.

The rain which had been indecisive all day decided to become a light rain once the pair reached Dexter Avenue. It was not a downpour, but it was just enough moisture to turn on the windshield wipers and leave them on intermittent to see.

Mase and Book ran down Dexter Avenue and found themselves on a long stretch of factory and dark warehouses and empty lots. The industrial area was a snaggle tooth smile of buildings. The emptiness of buildings was jarring. Mase knew as well as Book that the emptiness went back to years of believing in a dying industry.

Mase let up. Book looked left and right as they walked. Mase couldn't help looking back. He was waiting for someone or something.

"Why didn't we wait?"

"For what?"

"I don't know," Book said, uncertain. "It's raining."

Mase shook his head as an answer. Mase calculated. He looked back, expecting to see someone behind them. Thankfully, no one was trailing them.

"Come on," Mase said, taking a deep breath and pushing away from the bus stop and heading across Doris Street.

Mase looked at Book and shook his head, seeing a bus going in the opposite direction. The rain quickened and at the corner of Doris Street the two lost speed and came to a stop, getting their bearings. Mase looked back nervously.

Three more blocks, Mase calculated, and they would be at Oakman Boulevard and leaving the Brethren territory. Mase was looking back every so often. Book looked back when Mase looked back.

Just ahead of them was the neon sign advertising Bailey's Liquor Store. It was on the opposite side of the street. For a moment Mase thought they should cross the street so no one would pull up behind them unannounced.

"Hey, look there's a fire house," Book said, pointing toward the red brick building.

Mase looked up and examined the building with its doors closed. It called back a memory, long forgotten, for Mase.

Mase idly thought of when he was a little kid and gone to the fire department for a field trip. He was so happy to touch the fire engine truck and see the big firefighters boots. One of his classmates got to wear a fireman's helmet. For that day Mase thought about being a firefighter.

He shook the thought and memory from his head. He was not in elementary anymore. He was fifteen and full-grown. He and Book were runners. He and Book had to get back to Fisher Freeway. To get back they had to blend in. They just had to walk and run and look like they belonged.

The pair had to cross Chicago Boulevard and get to Corktown to be safe. The route was straight forward. The shortest route took the pair down Dexter Avenue and into and out of some unfriendly territory and through a few dicey neighborhoods before reaching Southwest Detroit.

The easiest route had to be down Scotten Avenue, but that meant cutting through DCG territory. Though, it was the sketchiest and most dangerous route, Mase did not really see another way.

The run that night was through a bunch of turf landmarks to Mase. He had made a run up to Motown Museum once before, but Happy's HQ was the farthest north he had ever been. Mase was a Southwest Detroit product. He liked it there. It was home.

So, Mase calculated the shortest route to Southwest Detroit was down Dexter Avenue and then over to Holmur Avenue and across East Edsel/Ford Freeway. Mase pictured the route and thought idly that when the pair got across East Edsel/Ford Freeway they were pretty safe, comparatively.

Mase figured, if they headed down Dexter and made it to Russell Woods, they would be safe from the DCG. Mase decided, if they got to Chicago Boulevard, they would be out of the DCG territory and then all they had to do was get to Core City and possibly skirt Southwest Detroit by cutting through Core City, but even that route was trouble.

Getting through Southwest Detroit was always difficult because of El Hefe and the Vatos. The Vatos were a dangerous group of gangsters trying to control their territory against three other Mexican gangs. The Vatos were fighting, at last count, Nuevo Caballeros, HEM (Hecha en Mexico) and Ciudad Ninos. Going through Southwest Detroit was always dangerous because there was no peace there after dark. There was an ongoing turf war all over Southwest Detroit.

Once they got to Core City, they still had to cross over Fisher Freeway and find Chocolate and his super-secret hideout. Getting to the super-secret hideout was the most dangerous part of the route. Chocolate's hideout was on the edge of the Vatos' territory. Mase and Book knew the backdoor entry into the hideout, thankfully because the Vatos ran most of Southwest Detroit.

At night, especially late night, in all sectors of the city, once all the tourists were off the streets, gangs, corner boys, jackers appeared. They did their business. They looked around for anyone who looked lost. They targeted runners, knowing many dealers had young runners delivering product or retrieving cash. Running at night was never easy but it was quick money.

"Mase?" Book said, touching his shoulder.

Book's voice broke Mase's thoughts. He looked at the boy beside him. Book was wiping the rain from his baby face. He looked at Mase curiously. Mase realized Book had asked him a question.

"What?" Mase asked.

"Why'd we run?" Book asked, curious.

"There was no point in waiting," Mase said. Mase looked back into the light rain and saw nothing. "Come on."

"What you mean?" Book asked.

Mase did not respond.

The misting rain became a light sprinkle, and the two boys ran looking for a place to get out of the rain. Both knew they could not stop until they returned to Chocolate's. Stopping was suicide. They had to keep moving. There were no young kids, runners, on the street after dark unless they were couriers. Everyone knew that. At least, everyone in the street game knew that Mase figured.

Mase looked back and watched as the darkness and rain replaced the memories of the rough handling by Happy Hammond and the Brethren and the warehouse in the midst of Brethren territory.

Crossing Oakman Boulevard put them that much closer to the end of the run. The two boys crossed Oakman Boulevard and walked on silently. Mase looked back. Book looked back a few seconds later.

The pair continued down Dexter Avenue. Mase pointed to a covered bus stop. The pair ran for the covering. Safely shielded from the suddenly intensifying rain the pair sat on the bus bench and waited out the rain, for a moment. Mase looked back in the direction they had come from as Book adjusted his backpack on his shoulders.

"We can't stay here," Mase said.

"I know," Book said.

"I was just saying," Mase said, climbing to his feet as the rain let up, just a little. "Come on."

"Why didn't we ask them for umbrellas or something before we got gone?" Book asked as the two jogged forward.

"They we're plotting," Mase said in slow breaths. "I heard something about teaching Chocolate a lesson." He reduced his speed and looked back again. Book eased up too.

"Wait," Book said reaching out as they walked past a tattoo shop on Dexter Avenue. "Thought this was supposed to be some sort of smoothing over delivery?"

"Maybe it was. I don't know. It just didn't feel right," Mase said. He looked back, cautiously.

"Why they want to teach Chocolate a lesson?"

"You asking me? I don't know how things work above my head. All I know, is the longer we stayed the more time they had to plot," Mase said with a shake of his head. "Right now, all that matters is we got what we were supposed to get. Now we got to get it back to Chocolate."

Mase and Book were walking for a moment. Mase looked back. Book looked back seeing Mase looking back.

"Wait, you telling me they were thinking about robbing or leaking or murking us?" Book asked.

"I ain't saying that. I ain't also *not* saying that. All that mattered was that we didn't stay up in there to find out," Mase said. The two boys began to run through the sprinkling rain.

The rain was indecisive. It was like some kid was playing with the faucet of a sink above them, the fifteen-year-old runner mused. The idea made Mase sneer.

The pair found themselves near the Greater New Jerusalem Missionary church when the rain sharpened. They sheltered there, as the rain amplified and went from drizzles to a downpour and then back to misting all under ten minutes.

"I thought we were *just* runners," Book said.

"Just runners? Sometimes it's good to be a runner. Most times it's just a simple run," Mase said, looking at the rain falling through the streetlights.

"We should have burners," Book said.

"Naw, fool, you get a burner and the worst thing happens is someone takes it away from you," Mase said with a shake of his head.

"I mean, I don't even have a knife." Book looked at Mase. "You still got your blade?"

He shook his head. "Remember Delmar took it?"

Book looked at Mase, confused.

"He never gave it back?"

"I never asked for it," Mase said.

Book shook his head. He looked around as the rain misted inches from them.

"We're good," Mase said with a smile. "Shit like this happens all the time."

"What?"

"It ain't that big a deal," Mase said, reaching out and slowing Book. He looked back and narrowed his eyes. He peered into the darkness. "We kind of got it easy because of the rain."

"Should have a weapon," Book said, decidedly.

Chapter 2.
Gangsta Gangsta

Two hours earlier, Delmar and Pancake had shown up in the Amicci's parking lot near Vernor Highway in a Mercedes Benz GLB SUV. The Mercedes had driven around the store and pulled up next to Book. Book watched silently. He did not run. He stood and watched as the passenger window slid down silently.

"Get in little nigguh," Delmar said from the front passenger side of the SUV. He was a thin eyed brown skinned man with a slender smile on his face. He had a trimmed two-inch high Afro framing his diamond-shaped face.

Book hesitated. Mase opened the rear passenger door opened and Book's hesitation vanished. Seeing Mase all Book's concern disappeared, and Book climbed in the SUV. Pancake was driving. The four drove down Vernor Highway to Junction Avenue and turned left toward Chocolate's complex.

"First," Delmar said, from the passenger seat behind his reflective sunglasses. "Either of you carrying?"

Book shook his head.

Mase reached into his jeans and pulled out a butterfly knife.

"Give me that," Delmar said, with a shake of his braided head. He snatched the knife from Mase and slipped it under the front seat. "All we need is for po-po to pull us over and one of you is carrying something. They always looking for a reason to end us."

Pancake stared at the pair of runners in the backseat and scowled.

"Drive Pan," Delmar said.

Pancake was so wide it looked like his shoulders would hit Delmar as he drove. The giant drove away from Amicci's and back toward Southwest Detroit. They crossed the Edsel freeway and turned right and toward a residential area. The SUV drove around the block and parked in the rear of one of the four houses at the end of the block.

The veterans climbed out and checked left and right before slipping into the back of the far building. Mase and Book followed behind.

Pancake led the way with Delmar behind. Pancake width and broad shoulders looked like they would brush either side of the hallway as he walked down a short hallway to what had been a kitchen. Delmar, just the opposite, was not half the size of Pancake. He was maybe six foot tall, but Pancake was a head taller.

Mase was maybe five foot something and not as wide as Delmar. Book was still growing and did not really care to measure his height. The four came under the eye of two men in the kitchen with sub machine guns.

Delmar and Pancake gestured and the man farthest away nodded and let the quartet pass. Mase and Book studied the two men. They entered the living room of the house and there in the living room was Chocolate's office. Book had to take a second look at the living room and entry into the redesigned offices of Chocolate Nathaniel. From the outside it looked like all the other houses on the bombed-out block, but inside it was state-of-the-art.

Two chiseled blocks of stone stood at the reinforced door, guarding the entrance to the second-floor entry to Chocolate Nathaniel's operations. Stairs led up but to get past the guards seemed nearly impossible. Sitting at a desk was a woman dressed in a tight blue dress which showed off her curves.

Book and Mase were guided past "Pam" to the offices of Chocolate Nathaniel. On the second floor of the house which looked out over the neighborhood was what looked for all intents and purposes like a boiler room you might see in a stockbroker's office. The difference was the dozen people sitting in the cubicles were not stockbrokers but drug distributors. They were stripped down to their underwear and under scrutiny by six armed guards. Everyone was wearing goggles and masks and wearing nitrile gloves. The boiler room was half the size of the second floor. The other half was an office for Chocolate.

Delmar and Pancake escorted Mase and Book to the door and waited.

"What do we do?" Mase asked.

"Knock," Delmar said with a shake of his head.

Mase knocked on the door.

"Come in," was the answer.

Mase and Book entered the office, leaving Delmar and Pancake in the exterior offices.

Chocolate Nathaniel was seated behind one of those desks which are carved up and designed like a piece of art. There was a big monitor on the desk and a phone. Behind the desk was this big picture of this old woman dressed in a denim outfit. She looked a lot like Chocolate Nathaniel.

"Listen. Mase you good. You and your sidekick are good?" Chocolate asked. "I need you to go to Happy's and drop these off," Chocolate pointed to the two backpacks beside his desk. "No later than nine. Make sure Happy gets it. When he gets his package, he's going to give you each a package to bring back to me. Simple," Chocolate said. "Any questions?"

"Naw, we got this," Mase said. "Just take this to Happy. Get a package from Happy. Bring what Happy gives you back to us."

Book agreed.

Pancake and Delmar drove them to the edge of Brethren territory.

"Cut down Dexter Ave and drop them off on Fullerton," Delmar said. "They can walk from there."

Mase and Book looked at each other, uncertain.

"It ain't that far," Delmar said. "We got to pick up something at the Motown Museum." He paused. "We'll see you back at the spot."

Delmar waved bye and he and Pancake drove away leaving them on Dexter Avenue. The two boys had walked down the street watching as the people slowly disappeared as they walked into the more industrial area, headed toward Brethren central.

It had taken a little more than a quarter of an hour before Mase and Book got to see Happy Hammond. They had been dropped off a little after nine o'clock.

Chapter 3.
Picking up the crew

Gerald had driven from his apartment to pick up Keyon first. He was the farthest away. Jayson wasn't that far from Gerald, but in the schoolteacher's mind, it seemed a better use of his time to pick up Keyon first.

Gerald didn't say it, but he always felt that Wendy, in her distinct way, was always too clingy and protective of Jayson. She was never happy to see Gerald or Keyon. She was like one of those cats that has territorial issues. She was cordial because of Jayson but not entirely friendly. Wendy was small smiles and cautious laughs when Gerald or Keyon or both were over, but it all seemed forced.

Gerald pulled up in front of Key's condo and fished out his phone. He scrolled through his messages and saw he had two messages from Gabriella already. Her first message was just Gabriella being Gabriella. It was a meme of a girl looking out a window, similar to how Gerald had last seen her. The second message was another meme of a little boy dressed in a suit looking back and mouthing the words: "Call me."

Gerald dialed Gabriella. The phone rang twice before his girlfriend answered.

"Gee? Where you at?" Gabriella asked.

"Just pulled up to Keyon's," Gerald said with a small grin.

"Okay, call me when you get to the restaurant," Gabriella said.

"Babe? You okay?" Gerald asked.

"Yeah, I'm just worried about you," Gabriella said.

"Ain't nothing going to happen to me. I'm with my boys." He paused. "I'm *about to be* with my boys. We always watch out for each other," Gerald said, correcting himself.

"I know, but I just would appreciate a check in," Gabriella said on the other end of the phone. "That ain't asking too much? Is it?"

"Naw, babe, it definitely is not too much to ask," Gerald said with a smile. "I'll text you when we get to Renaissance Center. I'll even text you when we get to Face Down." He paused. "Is that good enough?"

"Gee, don't make it sound like I'm being all... like that," Gabriella said.

"I ain't," Gerald said. "I get it. More importantly, sweetie, I appreciate you caring enough to want to know I'm okay. Ain't nothing wrong with that."

"Okay, good," Gabriella said.

"All right," Gerald said. "Now, I'm in front of Key's place. I was about to text him to come down and then we going to scoop up Jay. Do you want me to call you in between now and Joe Muer?"

"Don't play," Gabriella said, suddenly serious.

"I ain't. If you need me to let you know, then I'm going to let you know."

"I think once you are with Key and Jay I won't worry as much," Gabriella said. "I just know that you driving around in that car of yours draws a lot of attention." She paused and though she was being serious Gerald smirked. "I don't want to hear you got pulled over for something meaningless and find out you got shot by some jealous police."

"I hear you, babe," Gerald said. "I'm fine. We about to pick up Jay and then head to Joe Muer. We should be okay."

"All right," Gabriella said. "Don't forget to text me."

"Gotcha," Gerald said. "Love you," he added and waited.

"Love you too," Gabriella said.

He rung off.

Gerald felt a smile broaden on his face. He had a good woman in Gabriella.

Gerald checked his watch and texted Keyon.

Let's go. I'm downstairs.

On my way.

He texted Jay while he waited for Keyon to come down.

Though he and Keyon were always at odds Gerald loved his screwball friend. He had rough edges, but he was as loyal as a beagle.

Keyon for all his faults had a lot to do with bringing Gerald and Gabriella together.

As he waited in the M3, Gerald recalled it was because of Jayson that he had the BMW and the woman he loved because of Keyon. Gerald chuckled in the M3, at the influence his two closest friends had on his life.

While he was in college and Jay was trying to figure out how he was going to get his art degree the three friends got together. They were just months away from Keyon being deployed to Afghanistan. The three had one of their memorable discussions about cars to own.

"If I could afford anything I would get a Range Rover," Jayson said. "It is a beast of a SUV that offers all the comfort of a top end car but in a SUV body."

"No one drives SUVs in the city," Keyon said with a snicker.

"Yeah, I don't get those soccer moms and accountants in Hummers or Navigators," Gerald said with a laugh.

"Okay, if you are talking head turning city driving then I have to go for the BMW M3," Jay said. "It is easily the sleekest car out. It ain't one of those ridiculous cars that you buy and need to keep in a locked vault somewhere. You can drive the M3 and know that in a pinch you can skeet skirt out of trouble."

Gerald had laughed.

"I think if I get something it's going to be Italian. I like the Italian design," Keyon said.

"What you thinking? A Fiat? A Ferrari?"

"Ha. Ha. Ha," Keyon said, not amused.

Gerald's metallic black BMW M3 was his pride and joy. It was the first car he bought with his own money, after college. He took a year to decide on the car. He took another year to decide on the model. It was the third year out of college Gerald Cook finally bought the BMW and took it to the streets.

He and Keyon were on West Elizabeth Street and going to get a pizza at Michigan and Trumbull after Keyon had returned from Afghanistan and for some reason Jayson was unable to meet up. The two had small talked and as they were leaving and talking, Gerald had seen Gabriella and her group of friends. Keyon had looked at Gerald eyeing the pretty girl dressed in a blouse, jeans, and sneakers with a braided high ponytail.

"You going to make the move, Mackstrodamus?" Keyon asked, jokingly.

Gerald looked at Keyon and frowned.

Keyon smiled mischievously and walked to Gabriella and her three friends and introduced himself and then pointed to Gerald looking awkward and uncomfortable. Gabriella had giggled. Keyon gestured and Gerald had walked to the group of young women, just celebrating one of their friends' birthdays at Michigan and Trumbull. "Gabriella," Keyon said with a big smile. "This is my shy but brilliant friend Gerald Cook. I think you two might have a lot in common," he added and turned and started talking to the three other women.

A year later he was dating Gabriella and things were looking good. He never admitted it, but he gave a lot of credit to Jay and Keyon and his car for landing Gabriella.

At that moment Keyon came out of his condominium dressed as a guy about to be in charge of his own cannabis establishment. He was dressed in a silk Versace collared shirt, a black leather belt that had a buckle on it which might be worth Gerald's M3 tires, he was wearing black jeans and carrying a hooded sweatshirt which Gerald assumed was designer as well.

Climbing into the M3 Gerald's nostrils were assaulted by the heady fragrance of Keyon. He smelled like he had bathed in honey, smoked wood, rose petals and gardenias.

"Damn, man," Gerald said, frowning with the strong smell of cologne. "Did you leave any cologne at home?"

"Fuck you, hater," Keyon said, closing the car door and finding his seatbelt.

"I always enjoy your pithy conversations," Gerald said with a shake of his head.

"Comes with the job. Don't want me to be smelling like weed all night," Keyon said with a smile, buckling up.

"That's the new aphrodisiac," Gerald said, joking.

Keyon turned and smiled hard at Gerald and showed off his bottom gold grill.

"Key, can we not be all Hip Hop and Basketball tonight?" Gerald asked looking at Keyon only to close his eyes to the over-the-top nature of his friend.

"What? You don't like my grill?" Keyon asked, looking at his reflection on the sideview mirror.

"No, I don't like your grill," Gerald said. "I see that shit all day. Can you give it a break for tonight?"

Keyon reached across the space between the two and placed a hand on his longtime friend's shoulder, understandingly. He frowned. Keyon tilted his head a little to look Gerald in the eye before he spoke.

"Fuck you teach," Keyon said, with affected outrage. "I don't give one shit about what you have to deal with at school." He paused and rubbed the back of his head, looking out of the windshield. "You need to loosen up. Unbunch, muthafucka. No one cares if I have a grill or not. No one cares that you are a teacher. We just two nigguhs tonight. We just going out to support our boy. That's all. It ain't going to be on TV that you and me were seen on the streets after dark. This ain't no big production. We're just eating and then heading to Face Down. Shit ain't that complicated."

Gerald sat underneath the wheel of the M3 and closed his eyes to Key's words.

"Unbunch?" Gerald asked with a shake of his head. "I'm not all bunched up."

"Bullshit," Keyon said. He lifted his balled-up fist. "That's you. You need to relax or you're going to start shitting diamonds" Keyon smiled. "You so tight I wouldn't be surprised you don't have an ulcer."

"You know you can be a dick sometimes?"

"All day. It's who I am. I keep shit real," Keyon said with a smile.

Gerald pulled the M3 into traffic to pick up Jayson.

The music in the M3 was old school hip hop. Gerald loved the '80's and '90's era hip hop music and he and Keyon had no argument over the music as the M3 rolled toward Olde Towne to pick up Jayson.

"How's Gabi? She realize you the wrong nigguh for her yet?" Keyon asked, relaxing and leaning back in the front passenger seat.

Gerald laughed, mockingly. "She's fine," Gerald said as the pair skirted LaGrange and headed toward Collingwood Boulevard. Collingwood intersected with Cherry Street, but Gerald drove down Collingwood to turn left onto Victoria Place. He drove up the rear of Olde Towne and crossed Central Avenue headed to the tree lined Victoria Place. In the quiet neighborhood on the left was the two-block long apartment complex Gerald and Gabriella had tried to get into. Jayson lived just five minutes from that apartment complex on the other side of Victoria Place.

Gerald and Keyon pulled up to Jayson's house and both sat there looking at each other.

"You go and knock," Gerald said. "I got the car to watch," he added.

Keyon shook his head.

"Just call him," Keyon said, with a smile.

"You know that calling him only makes things worse. Go and get that fool," Gerald said, pushing Keyon toward the car door.

Keyon pushed back and shook his head.

"This is why I ain't with no one. No one about to run me," he said opening the car door and climbing out of the M3. He looked up and down the street and then closed the car door and headed to the three stone steps which led to Jayson's entrance to the home.

"This fool act like this girl is his momma or something," Keyon said under his breath, looking up to the big Bay window of the house above Jayson and Wendy's basement entrance. Keyon noted that the curtains were closed as they always were any time he came over after dark. Jayson had told Keyon that the old lady that lived above them was eighty and bright but a little skittish. She had allowed Jayson to move in to prevent any neighborhood burglaries his friend said.

Keyon walked down the short path and found himself at the red door of the entrance to Jayson's apartment.

Gerald sat in the car and listened to *Monie in the Middle*. He loved the British rapper's flow and delivery.

Monie in the middle (Where she at?) In the middle
   Yep, Monie's in the middle (Where that at?) In the middle

Monie in the middle (Where she at?) In the middle (Go Mon, Mon, what is she?) Monie in the middle

He was enjoying the hook when Jayson and Keyon returned.

Keyon climbed into the front seat. Jayson sat in the back and sulked, dressed in a collared shirt and blue jeans.

Gerald grinned from ear to ear and shook his head at Keyon and Jayson. Keyon seemed annoyed. Jayson was sulking in the back seat.

"What happened?"

"You know what happened," Keyon said. "That female can make the sun not want to come out."

"Just drive man," Jayson said from the backseat.

Gerald switched the music and pulled away from the curb listening to NWA.

You are now about to witness the strength of street knowledge.

In seconds, the car's dour mood flipped as NWA growled and dared everyone in the M3 not to bob their heads to their music.

They drove to Cherry Street and turned left and headed toward downtown.

When *Straight Outta Compton* ended Gerald grinned at the dance hit hip hop classic *Mo Money Mo Problems* bounced out of the car speakers.

By the time they neared downtown the M3 was more celebratory. Key's annoyance was gone. Jayson was rapping along with Biggie Smalls as the music switched and played the classic hip hop jam *Children's Story* by Slick Rick.

"This is my shit right here," Jayson said with a howl. "Love this song."

The trio proceeded to rap the entire song from X Avenue and X Boulevard all the way to downtown.

"Love Slick Rick," Jayson said. "I always wanted to go to England because of him."

"What were you going to do if you went there?" Keyon asked, looking back and not seeing Jayson.

"Hell, I don't know," Jayson said. "Hang out and get that accent. Maybe push up on some softies and listen to them talk like Slick Rick or Monie Love."

"Yeah, I would love to have hooked up with Monie Love," Gerald said, dreaming.

Just then EPMD's *You Got's To Chill* came on.

The trio listened and talked as Gerald weaved through the light traffic to the always busy and bustling Renaissance Center.

"Should I park down by Face Down?" Gerald asked as he slowed the M3.

"Hell no," Jayson said. "I ain't going to walk from there to Joe Muer. That's like a couple of miles, at least."

"Yeah, we ain't got to do all that," Keyon said, agreeing with Jayson.

Gerald reluctantly made his way to the busy entrance to the Renaissance Center. There were three restaurants there and easily one hundred people either walking in or walking out of those restaurants. At the entrance to the center there was also a riverside hotel. Being located on the River Walk there were hundreds of tourists milling about talking, laughing, holding hands, and taking pictures. In the circular entryway was a valet station with half a dozen men and women dressed in black pants, shoes and tie wearing red vests and smiling helping passengers in and out of their cars.

Gerald pulled into the parking entrance and immediately shook his head. He looked up and down the street as he pulled up behind another car.

"What you all of a sudden worried about your car?" Keyon asked.

"That's a soft move," Jayson said, agreeing with Keyon.

"Fuck you both, this ain't always the safest place," Gerald said pulling into the underground parking.

"If they want your car, they going to get your car. Ain't nothing an underground parking lot going to do," Keyon said.

"You would know," Gerald said.

"Ouch," Jayson said with a laugh.

Gerald found a parking spot in the underground parking lot, and everyone exited the car.

Keyon and Jayson looked back toward the ramp they had driven up, and Gerald whistled to get his friends attention. He pointed to an exit on the far side of the underground parking lot.

"Joe Muer is closer to this side," Gerald said as he walked to the stairs which led up to the main square. Keyon and Jayson followed.

Chapter 4.
On the run

Somewhere north of downtown and Joe Muer Mase redirected Book to turn onto Buena Vista and off Dexter Avenue. The two fast walked down the street with fifteen houses on the block to Holmur Avenue. It was wild to see a block with houses and no empty lots. Mase equated Detroit to a tornado's destruction. The tornado's destruction always seemed random, destroying some homes and sparing others for no apparent reason. Perhaps, the fifteen-year-old thought, there had been an invisible and unknown tornado that hit Detroit, but no one knew or recorded it.

The pair turned left on Holmur Avenue. On the short side of the block there were two single family homes. Mase expected that. Between the two houses was the alleyway where garages and garbage cans were found. Mase and Book walked down the quiet streets which looked like old school neighborhoods.

When the pair reached Richton Street there were six houses on the entire block. Of the half dozen only one seemed a big traditional single-family house with a porch and stairs leading to the porch. The idea of the tornado touching down came to mind.

Past that big house, on Monterey Street, there were just four houses clustered together in the emptiness of the entire block. On the opposite side of Monterey Street sat one house and only one house.

"I wouldn't live there," said Book.

Mase shook his head.

There was one big house on the other side of the alleyway, on the Duane Street side and Mase signaled for Book to turn on Duane Street. On either side of Duane there was emptiness. No houses. No garages. In the dark there were two houses at the top of the street before the two boys returned to Dexter Avenue.

"This is creepy," Book said.

"This is Detroit," Mase said, pointing toward the familiar Dexter Grinds sign. "Boom and bust, my granny used to say." He shook his head. "We walking through a horror movie or something."

Seeing the illuminated sign Mase pointed and continued toward Dexter Avenue. Mase and Book slowed their pace as they reached the avenue. Mase looked left and then right.

"We crossing?"

Mase shook his head. The teen stepped onto the sidewalk and started walking down the street. They had only gone a few steps before Mase looked back and Book imitated his actions. Mase adjusted the backpack on his shoulders and kept walking down Dexter Avenue.

They crossed Tuxedo and Book shook his head. They walked another empty block and Book reached out and pointed to the fenced off used car dealer. Across the street from the dealer was another block with no houses.

"We in no man's land?" Book asked.

"Keep your eyes open," Mase said to Book. Mase pointed out the gangland markers. On a trash dumpster were the red letters: HB.

Book and Mase walked on and just a block later Book pointed to a bus stop with the HB tagged on the back of the bench.

The rain seemed to get heavier as the pair passed another empty block and neared the neon sign of Food Farm. The pair stopped briefly at the steps of Saint Paul AME Zion Church. The pair sheltered under the awning of the church and watched cattycorner to them the sporadic street traffic passing in front of the empty Food Farm parking lot.

"Let's keep going," Mase said.

"It's starting to rain again," Book said, looking at the streetlights and the raindrops bulleting through the light.

"We got to keep moving," Mase said.

Book smirked.

The two had just crossed Longfellow when Mase and Book turned to see two cars going in the opposite direction turn around and head back toward them. One of the cars was a blacked-out Ford

Expedition. The other car was a tricked out electric blue Cadillac Escalade.

"We have to get off this street," Mase said. As the two SUVs sped up to turn around the pair ran diagonally across Dexter and Longfellow, through an empty lot which had been homes or apartments long ago to the back of five houses on Edison. Mase looked back and the two SUVs were following. The black SUV was racing down Dexter Avenue. The blue one was racing up Longfellow.

"Which way?"

"Well," Mase said, looking north and then south, uncertain. "We got to keep going south." He paused and grabbed Book by the shoulder and began walking like they were out for a night stroll across Edison Street. The two walked across the street and between the half dozen houses on that side of Edison.

Once in the fenceless backyards Mase moved with Book following stealthily back toward Dexter Avenue.

Behind them and on Edison they could hear the sound of a big block engines slowing and inching down the street.

Book reached out to Mase. Mase brushed Book's hand away with a frown.

The two boys were suddenly on a street with just four houses sitting next to one another in the middle of the block.

"We gonna run across Dexter and shake these fools," Mase said and before Book could complain he took off running.

The last house on the street was easily one hundred yards from the corner, but Mase did not care. He ran. He ran as fast as he could. He did not look back for Book or the SUVs. Mase simply ran.

At the corner, with cars running north and south, he did not slow, but boldly jumped into the traffic and darted across the oncoming traffic nearly getting hit half a dozen times. Book followed obediently in Mase's wake.

On the other side of Dexter Avenue Mase saw New McFall Brothers Funeral Home. Mase looked back and continued running. He ran through the parking lot of the funeral home and to the rear of the building. Book followed, trying to keep up. At the low fence which separated the property from nothing the pair hurdled it and landed back on Edison. There were three houses on the entire block. Instantly they ran west toward the end of the block and McQuade Street.

"Turn here," Mase said. "If we get below Columbus Street, we should knock off these fleas."

Mase guided Book across the deserted block back to Dexter Avenue. Book and Mase once on Dexter Avenue fast walked to Joy Road without seeing the Ford or the Cadillac. Book looked left and right for the SUVs.

"What do we do?" Book asked.

The rain increased. Mase pushed Book toward the corner. The pair crossed the street and stopped at Hook Fresh Fish & Chicken. They searched for a little shelter as the rain returned.

Under the slight awning and protection of the drive thru the pair paused, sheltered from the dampness falling from the dark skies. Both noticed the misting rain intensifying.

There was a line of eight or so cars waiting to get their orders and Mase scowled at the drivers and passengers' discomfort at seeing the two boys standing along the side of the building. Mase looked in the cars for familiar faces knowing no one would claim him. He had distanced himself from everyone who might have cared. Such was life.

Book adjusted his backpack and stretched, lost in his thoughts. Mase shook his head and for a moment wished he could go back in time and tell his younger self not to go down this path. Of course, he had no way to go back or stop himself from the path he was on.

"We close to Chicago Boulevard?" Book asked.

"Not yet," Mase said. He looked back and checked for anyone following them. "Let's keep going," Mase said. "Once we're on the other side of Chicago Boulevard I'll feel better."

Book agreed.

The pair crossed Joy Road and walked with Mase looking back a little more than before. Book was still checking the neighborhood and sidewalk ahead of them. Mase looked back and saw a pair of headlights racing down Dexter Avenue.

Mase looked around and noticed they had passed one of the two houses on the block. So, he grabbed Book and pulled him toward a tree in between the two houses as the low-slung car came speeding down the street playing its music loud. The car raced ahead and turned right on Pingree Street.

"You jumpy?" Book asked with a smile leaning against the tree.

"Got to be," Mase said pushing away from the tree's protection. "Never know who's coming for you."

Book did not respond. Instead, he just walked and found himself looking back a little more than before. He and Book stayed on Dexter Avenue and the dark and empty blocks of one or two and sometimes three houses on a block.

"Would you live here?" Book asked looking at the area they were in.

"I don't know," Mase said, unsure. "Maybe."

"This is the dead area," Book said as the pair crossed Whitney Street. It was odd to not see anyone out on their porches or on the streets. Mase looked up and down the street and like Book found the last ten blocks or so since Joy Road the streets were more like a post-apocalyptic movie.

"It's so weird," Book said. "I mean, I was trying to imagine blocks with houses." Book paused. "But I can't." He fell silent for a minute. "Do you think this city ever comes back?"

Mase looked at Book and shrugged. He scoffed at Book's youth. He was only two years younger than Mase, but it seemed like he was just a wide-eyed little baby boy all of a sudden.

"That's something that ain't got nothing to do with me. You know? It don't matter what I think," Mase said as he and Book crossed Northwestern Street and looked at a block which had only one building on the whole block. "Things are just so messed up here. Don't see how it really ever comes back. Things don't change for the good too often."

Chapter 5.
Scotten Avenue

On the northside of Detroit the pair of boys crossed Grand River Avenue and headed to Jeffries Freeway. Jeffries Freeway was a big freeway that was two three lane roads divided by a two-lane median strip. It was always busy, Mase noted. Many used Jeffries Freeway as an alternative to the busier roads into downtown.

Mase looked back in the dark for trouble. Book turned his head as well. It was his habit.

"You know, it's always the places where we can't run that we run into trouble?"

"Yeah," Book said in answer. "What's our choices?"

"There ain't none," Mase said, jogging across the road to the foot of the overpass.

Walking over the arch of the overpass they heard the distinctive sound of a rumbling engine revving behind them. The pair turned and saw a car idling at the stop light, maybe one hundred yards from them. The car was older and looked like a lowrider car. It was one of those low-profile cars with one of those grills which look all mean and fast, Mase thought.

"Is that trouble?"

"It ain't the tooth fairy," Mase said.

Mase pushed Book and began to run toward the far end of the overpass. Maybe five hundred feet from them was the next light at the foot of the overpass. Book looked back as he ran and nearly knocked Mase down.

"Watch it," Mase said, angrily.

"The light changed," Book said, pointing back.

Mase ignored Book and focused on reaching the stop light at the bottom of the overpass. Behind them came the dark lowrider as the pair ran against the light and traffic. The pair dodged the handful of cars crossing the intersection at that time of night.

The lowrider skidded to a stop at the light as Mase and Book, on the other side of the street, looked for a place to hide.

"We got to get off this street," Mase said and pushed Book toward Tireman Avenue. Before they could cross the street, they heard the sound of a big engine revving and a horn blowing as the lowrider tried to nose into the intersection and nearly hit a car crossing the intersection.

Instantly, Mase pushed Book toward the three trees on the corner of Tireman Avenue. Book first ran down the sidewalk only to turn and see Mase run between the trees and into the empty block behind them. Book turned and followed.

The lowrider tore across the intersection and made a sharp left turn only to hit its brakes. In the distance the boys heard screeching tires. Mase and Book ran across the space of four blocks and saw all of eight houses remaining in the area. Book looked back and saw the lowrider hop the curb.

The pair ran down the service road running parallel with Jeffries Freeway and as soon as Mase saw a slatted fence climbed over. Book was just steps behind Mase. The pair landed in a dark yard filled with plywood and pallets. Mase ducked down and pushed Book down as well.

"What should we do?"

"Quiet," Mase said.

A handful of seconds later the pair heard the roar of the muscle car and saw the dark silhouette of the vehicle race by. The car raced up the service road. In seconds, the rear lights disappeared out of sight.

Mase and Book climbed to their feet. Mase, standing on a wooden pallet looked for a moment like the captain of an invisible ship. Book laughed at the sight.

"What you laughing at?"

Book shook his head. He chuckled at Mase on top of the wooden pallet. Book looked left and right, expecting anything and everything.

The pair climbed back over the fence and continued walking, jogging down the service road. The pair doubled back and through the backyards for two blocks before popping back out and onto Scotten again.

"Why is this all Bourne Identity level?"

"I don't know," Mase said as they walked down Scotten, heading south. "Like I said, I think Happy and them were trying to set us up."

"Well, should you call Chocolate?"

"Naw, we promised him there would be no problems. Remember?"

Book nodded his head.

"They coming," Book said, reaching out for Mase's backpack.

Mase looked back and ran down the alleyway which separated the two sides of the blocks. The lowrider had found the alleyway and was racing down the gravel strewn stretch.

Mase redoubled his effort and ran toward the end of the street. Book followed. The pair cut across Scovel Place and through a couple of backyards before jumping over a fence and back onto Scotten Avenue.

Mase and Book crossed Scotten Avenue and paused beneath a group of trees and caught their breath.

"We good?" Book asked trying to catch his breath. Both boys were looking up and down the street for the lowrider.

Mase looked at Book and shook his head. He had his hands on his knees. He wasn't out of shape, but he was not a long-distance runner by any stretch of the imagination.

In the darkness the boys heard the sound of the lowrider's engine racing from a side street and both boys instinctively hid in the shadowiness of the trees they were resting beside.

On a street where twenty houses should have been there were only a dozen houses. The trees Book and Mase hid behind had sprung up on two empty lots. The lowrider tore down Moore Place only to brake hard again and reverse onto Scotten Avenue.

Mase and Book cut across the empty lots to Hartford Street.

On Hartford Street the two boys ran a block and paused at Milford Street checking for the lowrider. Just a block over was Scotten Avenue. Mase and Book watched the dark street as they walked down

Hartford. Book was looking left and right and back now. Mase continued to look back every so often as the two boys walked parallel to Scotten Avenue.

Mase and Book crossed back to Scotten Avenue after the lowrider disappeared.

They were on Milford Street. Mase shook his head as he saw the top of the block was supposed to be a neighborhood turned into an unofficial parking lot for a dozen cars. The pair did not slow or stop but kept walking down the relatively quiet street.

The pair returned to Scotten Avenue. They were walking down one of those half-filled blocks between Milford and Cobb Place when Book pulled on Mase.

Mase looked at Book, curious.

"You good?"

"How much farther?"

Mase didn't answer. Instead, he shrugged his shoulders and kept walking. "What difference does it make?" Mase asked as he walked. "We running. That's our job tonight." Mase paused. "The only thing that matters is getting these backpacks back to Chocolate."

The street seemed to stretch out forever in either direction. Every so often Mase or Book would look back to see if they were being followed. Book pouted in the dark, walking slowly behind.

In the dark, somewhere behind them, they heard the bassy sound of an engine in the dark. Mase whipped his head around. In the distance Mase thought he saw a late model car racing toward them.

Mase looked for a hiding place and the pair quickly rushed to a parked car on the side of the road and hid behind it. Book leaned against the car door hoping not to be seen. Mase, closer to the front of the parked car edged forward to see the muscle car race by. For the blur and darkness, the best Mase could determine was the car was maybe a Chevrolet or Buick, based on the sleek lines.

The car did not slow or stop but roared past the two boys. Mase looked at Book. Book climbed to his feet and watched the car disappear into the darkness.

Mase grabbed at Book and the younger boy shrugged off Mase's attempt to grab him. Mase walked on the sidewalk studying the street as he did. Book continued walking behind Mase.

"Look," Mase said, catching up with Book. "We can't be stupid. This is the business of this. We runners. We got a job and that's all." Mase paused. "We should be back in less than an hour. Maybe."

Book looked at Mase and frowned.

"What you mad?"

Book pouted.

"Okay, we can speed it up a little if we run a block and walk a block," Mase said, putting his hand on Book's shoulder. Book shrugged off Mase's hand. "At the next block we can run the block and walk the next one. That'll get us back quicker."

At the next block Book and Mase ran the entire block. The rain was a light sprinkle and though the rain spit the two boys did not seem to notice it as much. At the next block they walked.

"If we keep up this pace we should be back in the Southwest in under an hour," Mase said.

After running a few blocks, Book broke the silence.

"You ever been down south?"

"Why?" Mase asked.

"I was trying to figure out what Detroit reminds me of at night," Book said as an answer.

"It's like this down south?" Mase asked.

"Naw," Book said. "I think when I was down there, in Alabama, for a summer to see my grandmother it was...different."

Mase shook his head.

"I liked it down there. It's slow down there," Book said.

"Book? What are you talking about?" Mase asked, unsure what the thirteen-year-old was going on about.

Book got quiet, thinking. He was suddenly confused.

"I think I forgot your question," Book said finally.

"I didn't ask you a question," Mase laughed. "Come on."

The pair had a long run across the West Edsel Ford Service Road and then the East Edsel Ford Freeway. They took it at a jog. They ran all the way to West Warren Avenue before stopping or slowing down and walking to catch their breath.

"Okay, I remember what I was talking about," Book said. "The city is like down south."

Mase did not speak. He waited.

"I think it's like down south when everyone left and there was all this space and people wanted to live anywhere but there. My Gram told me that a lot of people moved out of the south and whole neighborhoods were empty." Book paused. "I think it's sort of like that."

Mase grinned. He did not want to offer his opinion.

"What?" Book asked.

"Just thinking. You know," Mase said with a smirk. "Trying to get back to Chocolate in one piece and not letting no one jack us."

"No, I mean about the city?" Book asked. He was suddenly by Mase's elbow.

Mase walked on silently.

"I know you have to be thinking how crazy it is to walk through all this," Book said, gesturing toward the neighborhood and the empty lots where houses used to stand. "It's like some zombie movie without the zombies or something."

Mase grinned.

"No," Book said with a smile, rethinking his initial idea. "It's like the end of the world and no one told anyone in Detroit."

Mase chuckled. He shook his head at Book.

"It's like a tornado hit," Mase said.

Book frowned, confused.

Mase eventually told Book his tornado idea.

"You mean like the Wizard of Oz?"

Mase shook his head.

A few blocks before they reached Buchanan the growl of a car tore through the night. It seemed close. Mase ducked instinctively, like there had been shots fired. Book ducked too because Mase had.

The car, bright red and mean came tearing down the street and Mase and Book stepped into the darkness and protection of the trees growing near the sidewalk.

Mase and Book watched as the red car raced down Scotten Avenue not slowing or seeming to be looking for the two runners.

"False alarm?"

"Yeah, I guess," Mase said to Book.

Chapter 6.
Joe Muer

Joe Muer was a Detroit premier seafood restaurant. The restaurant had one of the best riverfront views in the city. One of the distinctive features of Joe Muer's was their piano bar. Built in 1929 the restaurant also featured a lounge and Ship and Riverfront Room.

"Gentlemen," the waiter said, once he appeared.

The three friends turned their attention to the waiter dressed in a white collared shirt, black trousers, and black apron.

"Welcome to Joe Muer," the waiter said. He was a young and rugged looking man with blonde hair and blue eyes. They were guided to the always busy side of the restaurant with the river side view and seated.

Gerald Cook took the menu the waiter offered and shook his head for a drink. He didn't want a drink right then. Instead, he just wanted to hang out with his friends.

The trio sat and talked about Jayson's new job.

"So, tell me what idiot hired you?" Keyon asked.

"I'm not going to dignify that question with a sensible answer," Jayson said with a smile to Keyon. "I was hired by MGM Grand."

"You mean the movie studio?"

"Well, sort of," Jayson said with a grin.

Gerald and Keyon's eyes bugged. Keyon knew Jayson got a job, but his friend hadn't told him the company was the MGM Grand.

"I know what it sounds like but I'm just working at the MGM Grand Hotel as their video assistant. It's a glorified assistant to one of the directors there. Nothing groundbreaking."

"Fuck that," Keyon said. "It's definitely groundbreaking."

"Yeah, congrats," Gerald said with a smile. "Well deserved." Gerald took a pause. "Do you get a deal on hotel rooms?"

"I guess," Jayson said to Gerald.

"I heard they don't hire us, too often," Keyon said, pointing to the back of his hand. He was sipping a beer.

"Well, that obviously ain't true," Jayson said, pointing at himself.

"Wait you trying to tell me there's a bunch of brothers and sisters at MGM Grand?"

"Well, not a bunch, maybe a sprinkling," Jayson said with a chuckle.

They sat, drank, and talked. Keyon was the quiet and brooding one. Yet, that night, in Joe Muer, he was surprisingly lighter and less subdued.

"You know I can't really remember the last time I came here," Keyon said, with a laugh.

"You probably come down here a lot more than either of us," Gerald said with a grin.

"Of the three of us, you two definitely have been here more than me," Jayson said with a chuckle.

"I think that this place always felt a little off limits to me, for some reason," Gerald said.

"Don't know why," Keyon said. "They take cash, card and credit, just like everyone else."

"You know what I mean," Gerald said to Jayson.

"I know what you mean," Jayson said, with a nod.

"Man, I'm not going to let you put a damper on the night," Keyon said. "We are celebrating." He paused and looked at Gerald. "Besides, you picked the restaurant."

"Yeah, I did do that," Gerald said with a sheepish smile.

As they finished their celebratory meal Gerald spoke.

"You know I'm proud of you, Jay," Gerald said with a smile.

"Yeah, me too," Keyon said, wiping at his mouth.

"Man, I don't know why. I mean, I am smart, and I know my shit."

"Yeah, that ain't always enough," Gerald said.

The restaurant was loud and lively. Beautiful women dressed in bright colors and expensive fabrics moved back and forth amongst the tables. Men, young and old, drank and ate as the wait staff scurried here and there.

The table waiter reappeared. Gerald smiled at the waiter. Keyon had his menu in his hand. Jayson was ready to order.

The three all ordered. Gerald ordered a lemonade and water. Jayson ordered a Gin and tonic. Keyon ordered a Sierra Nevada Pale Ale.

"Hey, I got to go to the little boy's room," Gerald said, climbing to his feet. He scanned the restaurant and made his way to the toilet. When he returned to the table, he knew Keyon and Jayson were up to something.

"What did you two do?" Gerald asked, skeptically.

Keyon and Jayson looked at Gerald shocked. Before Gerald could figure up what his two oldest friends were up to the server and waiter returned with their food.

Jayson and Keyon eyed each other. Jayson smirked. Keyon and Jayson watched as Gerald sipped his beer. Keyon shook his head.

"So, we were talking and he and I had a bet," Jayson said.

"This is bad, already," Gerald said, with a shake of his head at his two friends.

"We want to know how you out after dark on a school night?"

"My money is on you getting shit canned or about to be shit canned," Keyon said with an evil smile.

Gerald shook his head.

"I thought that teachers weren't allowed to... I don't know. Go out? Have fun?" Keyon asked.

"Ain't you worried about a piss test or drug test in the morning?" Jayson asked.

"Why?" Gerald asked.

Jayson pointed to the beer Gerald had in front of him. Keyon looked at Gerald, curious. Gerald shook his head.

"I can have a drink and still be a teacher," Gerald said.

"Don't they drug test teachers and whatnot?" Keyon asked.

"Nope," Gerald said with a smile. "I mean, maybe. I don't know." He paused and looked at Keyon. "Why would they need to drug test me?"

Jayson looked at Gerald quizzically. He pointed to the beer again. Gerald shook his head at Jayson.

"So, you didn't get fired?" Keyon asked.

"What? No." Gerald said with a shake of his head.

Keyon leaned forward, looking at Gerald.

"I mean, I hear teachers get fired left and right for fucking around," Keyon said.

"What?" Gerald asked, looking at Keyon. He frowned at his lifelong friend. "Firstly, I told you that. But I ain't got to sweat that. You know me. I ain't fucking around. I'm good at what I do."

"Yeah," Jayson said with a nod.

"So, is there a holiday or something tomorrow?" Keyon asked.

"Is it hug a teacher day tomorrow or something?" Jayson asked with a chuckle.

Gerald shook his head at his friends sitting at the table with him. He loved Jayson and Keyon, but they never listened to him anytime he talked about school. They only listened to the war stories. They zoned out when he talked about the daily routine and work he did. He recalled anytime he started talking about his job and scope and pressures of local and state requirements going on in school their eyes seemed to glaze over.

For a moment, Gerald thought to make up something fantastic. Maybe he had to go to court? Maybe he was doing a paternity test? The crazier the better. He shook the fantastic from his thoughts.

"Every so often we are required to do a professional development," Gerald said. He looked at his two friends who were looking at him as if he had just spoken Russian. He scowled and shook his head. "I have a conference tomorrow and no kids. Paid day working without kids," Gerald said with a grin, adding for clarity. "No school for the kids tomorrow."

"So, you get to let your nuts hang a little tonight," Keyon said.

Gerald shook his head and laughed.

"Yeah, I suppose."

"Just a little," Jayson said with a laugh, looking at Gerald.

Chapter 7.
No man's land

The two boys wearing their bright backpacks kept their run a block, walk a block routine up. They were still on Scotten Avenue and in this part of the city there were no homes on either side of the street. There hadn't been houses for two or three blocks. In the darkness, Mase could not help but see trees reclaiming the empty house lots.

From Buchanan to Magnolia, seven blocks, there were four houses combined on that stretch of road. The boys were walking between Jackson and Magnolia Street when Book looked at Mase curiously.

"What?" Mase asked the boy next to him.

"Where are all the corner boys?"

Mase shook his head. "There's no corner boys where there's no people," Mase said. "The corner boys would be crazy to post up out here. Ain't nobody around. Think they going to be closer to downtown."

"But—" Book said, twisting his lips and thinking.

"Think about it. It's raining. Corner boys are out rain or snow."

Book nodded his head.

"We sort of got a pass," Mase said with a grin.

To the right of them was an empty space which could hold two traditional houses but was being used as an unofficial trailer parking spot. The open space held a dozen semi-trailers. There was room enough for at least four times as many.

"We ain't seen nobody out of the streets in a while."

Mase shrugged off Book's comment.

Chappell Steel factory was on corner of Magnolia Street and Scotten Avenue. The factory ran the entire length of the block until Torrey Avenue.

Of course, Mase thought, as soon as Book made that comment there was the sound of a car's tires skidding behind them. The two boys looked back and there was a late model car making a U-turn in the middle of the street.

"Damn," Mase said, looking for a place to hide.

Book grabbed Mase to Mase's surprise. The younger boy pulled Mase forward.

"I know what to do," Book said.

Mase looked back and not having a lot of options followed Book. The white shiny backpack swung left and right as Book ran. Mase looked and thought Book was going to try and make it to the underpass. At the underpass Book made a hard right and into what was a ditch that led to a strip of grass that most would overlook.

Book and Mase slid down the grass slope into the dark. Book instantly turned toward the darkness and Mase checking for the car was slow to turn and look into the darkness. In the darkness and murkiness Mase saw movement. He recoiled instinctually.

Immediately the darkness moved and coalesced into eyes, faces and bodies of men, women and children and their dogs, cats and whatever else was living beneath the freeway above. Just under the lip of the freeway. Mase watched the huddled group of people there.

By the underpass was a homeless camp with dozens of tents and a handful of cars parked along the strip of grass and against a tall chain link fence that separated the strip from a business on the other side. Book and Mase counted three vans and a RV lodged by the underpass. The camp bristled with Mase and Book's arrival.

Sixty plus eyes were focused on the two boys. Four or five dogs barked in the darkness.

"We better cut through here," Book said.

Mase nodded his head and looked at the campers looking at him and Book.

There were several families, or what looked like families under the freeway. There were kids younger than Mase and Book sitting in the interior of their cars, tents, or shelters.

"Glad you saw this," Mase said as the two boys maneuvered through the homeless camp.

"Well, it ain't actually a shortcut," Book said, wiping the rain from his face as they picked their way through the camp. Mase walked watching the scowling faces of men, women, and children as they passed.

"What you mean?"

"Well, we cut across here and then we can cross Michigan Ave," Book said. "So, we going to be a little out of the way going this way."

"It ain't that big a deal," Mase said and shrugged.

The two boys pushed through the camp and though there were harsh looks and words they made it out without any issues.

"Who in the fuck do you think you are to walk through my private property," a chestnut woman with a bony face, big eyes and knotted hair said. She was standing on the running board of her car. The car looked like it hadn't run for years.

"Don't say nothing," Mase said to Book.

"Fuck you," Book said all angry.

"Fuck you," the woman said, dressed in a dirty T-shirt and jeans.

Mase grabbed Book and pulled him along.

Mase and Book watched the camp as they walked away and toward Michigan Avenue. The commotion was over as quickly as it had begun and in a few minutes Book and Mase were on Michigan Avenue.

They climbed onto the busy street and walked down to Scotten Avenue. They crossed the eight lanes of Michigan Avenue and dropped back on Scotten Avenue.

"So, we should be good from here all the way to the other side of the industrial park."

"Well, we should be good but once we get in there ain't too many places to hide. Lots of fences. Lots of wide spaces. It's built for big old tractors and trailers," Mase said.

Book nodded his head.

They entered the industrial area which began at Chappell Steel and stretched for over a mile all the way to the 24-Hour Tow yard. They would have to walk for nearly thirty minutes to reach the other side. As they walked down the overpass Mase and Book saw the end of a gigantic parking lot with dozens upon dozens of tractor trailers. A tall chain link fence ran the length of the area.

"It doesn't look friendly," Book said.

Behind the two boys, as silent as death, slid another dark car. It was Mase who saw the car's lights appear at the top of the overpass.

"Who's that?"

Mase looked at Book and back to the car.

"Run," Mase yelled, and he and Book ran toward the end of the street and the gate and tried to enter the gate. Mase and Book ran and shook the ten-foot-high gate looking for a way in.

"Cross the street," Mase yelled. He and Book crossed the wide street and again found themselves in front of a ten-foot-high fence which enclosed another parking lot filled with twenty semi-truck trailers.

Behind the two boys flashed the car lights descending the ramp into the industrial park area. Book and Mase whipped their heads around and desperately sought a way into the tractor trailer parking lot as the unknown car came off the overpass and into the industrial park.

In a corner of the fencing Book kicked and the fencing gave way just enough to squeeze underneath. Book pushed himself under the fencing and once on the other side climbed to his feet and called out to Mase.

Mase turned and saw Book on the other side of the fencing. He ran to the opposite side of the fence and Book pulled and Mase saw how the little boy had entered. Mase scrambled under the fencing as the pair heard the engine and car speeding toward them.

Mase and Book on the other side of the fence hid beneath one of the trailers as the car, a silver Honda, inched along the road. The car's engine sounded bigger than the car was.

It seemed close, maybe, Mase guessed, just a few feet from them, but that was not possible.

"What we doing?"

"Waiting," Mase said.

"How long?"

"Just a few minutes," Mase said. "They ain't going to stick around if they don't see us." Mase added, "I guess they turn around or keep going not seeing us."

"How will we know what they do?"

"I don't know," Mase said with a shrug of his shoulders. "Let's just take a minute to breath and then deal with everything else."

Book squatted and then knelt under the trailer. It was drier than out in the drizzle of the night. Just to the left and right of Book, feet away, the raindrops seemed to become mini goblets of water. Mase looked amused at the sight of the rain and Book turning around beneath the trailer like a cat or dog patting down where it was about to lay.

The big-eyed boy eventually sat on the still dry ground while the rain seemed to slacken. The big raindrops disappeared, and he and Book waited. Mase watched Book's squatting, kneeling, and then sitting and shook his head.

Mase looked around the trailer they were under, waiting for the car to turn around.

A few minutes later and the car raced back through the night, up the overpass and into the dark. Book looked to Mase. Mase pouted, thinking.

The pair of boys climbed out from under the trailer and made their way to the fence and their exit. Book looked at Mase.

"What do we do?"

"What do you mean?"

"I mean, is this worth a band?"

"Hell, yeah," Mase said, turning on his heels and beginning to walk down the street on the left side of Scotten Avenue, going against the oncoming traffic.

Mase only walked a few feet when he turned and looked at Book following but not bouncing along like before. Mase studied Book, understanding.

"Look, this is the life," Mase said. "We runners. We ain't corner boys. We ain't trigger boys either." He paused, still walking, and reaching out for Book. Grabbing a handful of Book's sweatshirt Mase pulled him along. "We stay in this long enough and we move up.

This ain't TV or a movie. This is real deal. If you ain't built for it, then you might want to go back and try something else."

Book shook Mase's grip, annoyed.

"What else is there?" Book asked scornfully. "I just didn't think that it would be like..." he trailed off.

"The bigger the risk the more we get. This is a big deal. Chocolate relying on us. We get this run back to him and we might be full-time spotters or corner boys."

"I don't want to be no corner boy," Book said. "They get popped too easy."

Mase was about to say something when he noticed they were near the underpass which would put them on the edge of the 24-Hour Tow yard and Southwest Detroit. He moved cautiously as he and Book approached the underpass.

"What you thinking?"

"I'm thinking this is a perfect place to get jumped," Mase said, looking left and right for an alternative route.

"Wait, you think someone's in there waiting for us?" Book asked.

Mase looked at Book and smiled mirthlessly.

"I've been fifty-fifty with the whole run and hide and worry thing, but I don't think there's anyone in there waiting for us," Book said with a grin. "I mean, they would have been in there for a long time waiting. Ain't nobody that stupid." Book shook his head. "I mean, we haven't seen anyone on the streets in a long time."

"I suppose you're right," Mase said, giving into Book's logic. Mase agreed reluctantly and gave Book that one. He chuckled at his paranoia.

Chapter 8.
Nearly Ten

The first appetizer was heart of romaine salad. The salad was delicious and a light treat. As the trio finished their salads a server and the waiter returned to the table with their meals.

"Bon Appetit," the waiter said, and walked away from the table.

Gerald had a tender chicken breast and wild mushroom picatta entrée. It sat upon a bed of risotto, shitake mushrooms and was bathed in wine, garlic, capers and a demi glaze. The meal looked like it had been cut out of a food magazine.

Jayson ordered a traditional salmon Alla Bella. The dish was a delicate mix of mushrooms, risotto and fresh vegetables and a fresh piece of salmon on the plate.

Keyon, the seafood lover, ordered Joe Muer seafood sauté. The plate arrived with a large helping of Pacific prawns, scallops and Dungeness crab legs sitting in a wine, garlic, and butter sauce. Keyon could only smile at the seafood treat before him.

The three friends ate. The meal was a welcome break for all three.

"This is a treat," Gerald said.

"Yeah, it's nice to just be out with my boys," Jayson said with a smile.

Keyon only nodded.

The waiter returned and asked if they wanted dessert. Jayson ordered a coffee. Keyon sipped at his water. Gerald was finishing off his beer.

The waiter returned with the bill.

After dinner, the trio of Jayson, Keyon and Gerald climbed back in the M3 and drove down the street, away from downtown, and toward the industrial district which bordered on the edge of Corktown and the Westside Industrial side of downtown. The shift from lofts and bars and well-lit places was quick and only three or four blocks past TCF Center, the last big landmark closest to GM Renaissance Center fell away and was replaced with the spotty darkness of Southwest Detroit.

Three more blocks from TCF Center and all the artifice of downtown Detroit seemed miles away. Gone were the neon and nice cars. Replaced in this part of the dim section between West Fort Street and West Jefferson Avenue were semi-trucks and trailers. Warehouse, businesses sat behind chain link fences stretched down the street Gerald and his two friends drove down.

The three friends drove down West Lafayette and their old stomping grounds. They had all gone to Amelia Earhart Middle School.

A few blocks before Clark Street Gerald parked the M3 just a few doors down from the Face Down bar and the three friends walked maybe one hundred yards to the dark and dingy saloon.

"How come you ain't worried about your car down here?"

"I don't know," Gerald said with a shrug of his shoulders. "I know people down here."

"You stupid," Keyon said. "Because you know people down here you should be on guard that much more."

Gerald twisted his lips and shook his head deciding not to argue.

Jayson walked into the small, local bar. Keyon followed with Gerald last. They were greeted by the bartender, behind the bar, and about half a dozen customers drinking at the bar. Scanning the interior Jayson was the first to notice there was a table open near the middle of the bar. He walked to the open table and sat down. Keyon followed. Gerald was the last to make his way to the table under the watchful eyes of the bartender and the barmaid.

The bartender, a ruddy faced white man dressed in a long-sleeved soiled shirt, looked up and stared the three into the bar. He was a big man, across his chest, and though his ice blue eyes did not speak they reflected his icy expression as the three friends walked into the small bar.

The bartender only shook his head and wiped down the long bar dominated the small bar. In the bar were maybe half a dozen customers. All of them looked as the three young men entered.

"I always forget about the weirdness that goes on when we enter," Jayson said to Gerald.

"Yeah, it's like we went back in time or something," Gerald said.

"Aw, they just sometimes forget that we was freed from the plantation," Keyon said with a laugh, pushing past the two who were eyeing the others in the all-white bar. Keyon grinned and stepped forward.

The barmaid cut her eyes toward the three entering the bar and studied the group. She recognized them. She observed to the bartender and looked to the two men at the table she was cleaning up.

The three had been coming to the bar on and off for a couple of years the barmaid recalled. They appeared, drank, never caused any trouble, and left usually leaving a decent tip. No problems from this group, she thought.

The barmaid was in her late forties and looked like she was nearly sixty. Her beauty, whatever there was, had dissipated like her hopes and dreams long ago. Her face was lined and angular. The barmaid's blonde hair was pulled back into a soft bun of hair held in place with half a dozen barrettes.

Keyon pointed out an open table and crossed to it with his friends behind. Jayson tipped his chair and the shells of peanuts or whatever fell to the floor. Gerald hesitated seeing the table had not been cleaned off.

Keyon walked to the table and swept the remains of whatever had been on the tabletop to the floor before sitting down unconcerned. Gerald looked at Keyon surprised.

"What?"

"Nothing," Gerald said.

Jayson shook his head.

Gerald watched as the woman slowly approached the three at the small round table. Her round blue eyes sat above a sharp beak of a nose. Her thin lips were just a line as she stopped and looked down on the three men.

"You know what you want?"

"Hello to you too," Keyon said with an emotionless smile.

The barmaid looked to Keyon and silently stared daggers at him.

"What do you have on draft?"

The angular woman looked annoyed. She studied Gerald and then the others.

"We have just three," the barmaid said, her voice a rasp. "There's Three Floyds Zombie Dust from Indiana. There's Sierra Nevada Pale Ale. That's from California. And we have Bell's Two Hearted Ale from right here in Michigan by way of Seattle."

"I'll take a Zombie Dust," Gerald said with a nod.

"Hey, easy tiger," Keyon said to Gerald. "That's two beers in one night." He looked at Gerald seriously. "Remember you are the designated driver."

"Yeah, I know," Gerald said to Keyon. He turned to the barmaid. "I just want one drink. Cut me off after the one Zombie Dust."

The barmaid smirked but did not say anything.

"Okay," Jayson said, drawing the barmaid's attention. "Yeah, I'll take one of those Zombie beers too," Jayson said, looking back toward the jukebox, in the rear of the bar.

"Hey, can I have a tequila shot?" Keyon asked.

The woman spun on her heels and walked to the bar.

"Always like coming here," Jayson said. "They are so friendly and welcoming."

"Shut up, man," Gerald said, with a chuckle. "It's the Face Down and it's our tradition."

"Yeah, I know, but sometimes we need to make our own traditions."

Keyon looked around the bar and noticed there were mostly men in the Face Down. Other than the barmaid there were two women in the whole place.

"I'm going to try my luck," Jayson said, climbing to his feet.

Keyon and Gerald watched as Jayson walked toward the rear of the bar and veered a little to the right into a dark corner.

"I don't know how they can do it," Gerald said to Keyon.

"Do what?"

"Have a slot machine in their bar," Gerald said watching the men drinking and talking at the bar and tables near them.

"Simple, man," Keyon said, with a look to the bar. "They are connected in some way. They greasing someone's palm so that slot is never noticed." He paused, thinking. "It's sort of how the cannabis trade is working nowadays, according to my boss."

"I get the whole connection thing, but I just don't get how no one has gotten upset and tried to shut them down?"

"I mean they have to be licensed," Gerald said.

"Not everyone that is a criminal is always caught," Keyon said. "For some its who you know not what you know. I thought you would know that teach," Keyon added.

"I guess. I just thought that the basic rules applied to everyone," Gerald said.

Keyon brightened at Gerald's words.

A few minutes later the barmaid was back with the drinks. Keyon paid for the first round. Jayson seeing the drinks arrive returned to the table with a handful of quarters.

"How's your luck?"

"Not bad," Jayson said to Gerald.

"Hey, I got the first round, but I ain't paying for another round unless I get my round paid for," Keyon said to the back of Jayson, who was watching the dark corner.

"Come on Key, you know you are fat with cash," Jayson said with a smile. "Why you tripping about paying for a round?"

Gerald looked evenly at Keyon.

"That's *your* friend," Gerald said to Keyon.

"He's more *your* friend than mine," Keyon said with a shake of his head.

"Damn, that is a beer," Jayson said, blinking a little more than he normally did. "It has a bit of a kick."

Gerald sipped his beer and winced at the kick of the Zombie Dust.

"That's what you get for ordering something called Zombie Juice," Keyon said.

"Zombie Dust," Gerald corrected.

Keyon smirked at Gerald and threw back his tequila shot and gestured to the barmaid for another. He shook his head after the alcohol splashed the back of his throat and started to warm his insides. Keyon closed his eyes to the liquid fire suddenly burning inside of him.

Gerald peeled off two twenties and sat them on the table for the second round.

"Hey, I got to go to the little boy's room," Gerald said, climbing to his feet. He scanned the small bar and saw the sign for the men's room. He headed to the rear of the bar and on the opposite side of the bar from Jayson was the only two working toilets in Face Down. Well, Gerald assumed the women's restroom was functioning. He pushed open the black door and entered the graffiti dominated interior of the space held one sink, a porcelain trough and two stalls which had to hold the two toilets. The black and white tiled floor was covered in a thin layer of water. At least, that is what Gerald wanted to believe. He stepped to the porcelain trough and relieved himself.

Chapter 9.
Industrial Park

The boys drew close to the underpass and on either side, there were a set of stone steps and a black rail used to keep people from falling into the street beneath the underpass. Mase looked for as far as he could and saw the street on the other side of the underpass.

"Pick a side," Book said. Mase blinked, finding Book by his side. Mase hesitated. Book pushed off and went to the right side of the underpass.

"Last one through owes the other a hundy," Book said and jumped up and onto the steps and began running through the darkened underpass.

Mase leaped onto the stone steps and grabbed the railing to steady himself. He and Book were suddenly six feet off the street and on a hundred-foot-long stone path. Mase began running seeing the white shiny, plastic backpack already bouncing along the passageway on the far side of the street.

The race through the underpass took less than a minute and Book nearly won. The two had run and though Book had an early lead Mase caught Book. It seemed the race was going to be a tie until Mase jumped from the end of the stone path to the street below and arrived a few seconds ahead of Book.

The pair caught their breath leaning on the chain link fence which began as soon as they were out of the underpass. On the other side of the street there was emptiness in the darkness. There were no cars, houses, buildings there. A block over Mase and Book could see the low-slung shape of a building.

"This might be a zombie movie we're in and we just don't know it," Book said, standing up and filling his lungs with air.

"Shut up," Mase said as they continued down Scotten Avenue. The chain link fence stretched for at least three blocks. There was a rolling gate which was locked as the two boys walked past it. Old cars, foreign cars, newer cars were parked near the fence Mase and Book noticed. They walked past the Deming Street signpost where the rolling gate stood and loitered just long enough to read the sign: Boulevard & Trumbull Towing.

The boys continued down Scotten to Brandon Street.

Between Brandon and Toledo Street there were only five houses on a street which should have had at least twenty houses.

"I would never live in this neighborhood," Book said as they crossed Toledo Street and saw the first corner boys standing on Scotten Avenue just a block away.

"You see what's ahead?"

Book looked and saw the group of four boys standing on the corner and looking in Book and Mase's direction.

"What we going to do?"

Mase shook his head as an answer.

They were halfway between Toledo and Wolff Street and Mase noticed there were three cars parked along the curb. He pulled Book to the left and into the empty lot where a house should have been. Two of the corner boys broke off from the corner and began running toward Mase and Book.

"They coming," Book said. Mase nodded, thinking.

Looking around Mase calculated a route through the six houses on the block to the next street over.

"Come on," Mase said, and he back pedaled and ran along the side of the house they were closest to and into the darkness. Book ran, just behind Mase.

"They still coming?"

"Yep," Book said between breaths.

"How many?"

"Just two," Book said.

"That ain't good," Mase said as they ran from Scotten Avenue to the dark street where four cars were parked. Mase looked left and right and could not believe there were just three houses on the whole block. Mase ran across street and through the patch of trees on the side of the street that had six houses. Mase and Book ran to the alleyway between the nameless streets and only paused long enough to look back.

"They still following?"

"Don't know. Don't see 'em," Book said, leaning against one of the trees to catch his breath.

Mase looked into the darkness but saw nothing. He listened but heard nothing. He looked at Book and his shiny, plastic backpack and tried to think.

"What we do?"

Mase didn't answer immediately. He had to think. He had to orient himself. He needed to know where they were.

He looked for landmarks. All he knew was they had been on Scotten Avenue but wasn't sure how many blocks they had ran to stop in the alleyway. Mase took a deep breath and straightened up letting his lungs fill with fresh air. They were safe for the moment, Mase decided, hiding in the patch of trees which had taken over half of the unknown block.

"Come on. We need to figure out where we are," Mase said and walked away from Scotten Avenue and to the street just on the other side of the alleyway.

Mase cautiously stepped out and onto the dark street and looked left and right and then back to figure if they were closer to West Grand Boulevard or Hubbard Street. Mase and Book walked south and noted the three houses on the block they were on.

At the corner, Mase and Book saw the street sign that identified the street they were on as Vinewood. There was a short street that was labeled Shady Lane.

"So, what are we doing?"

"Well, we got to get to Fisher at some point," Mase said. "Now that we are all the way over here it might be easier to just shoot down Vinewood until we get to West Lafayette Street and then take that to Chocolate's spot."

Book silently agreed.

Mase took a moment. He wondered if he had said that they were going to wait for aliens to pick them up if Book would have done anything differently?

Mase and Book continued southward.

"We ain't going to cut through Mexico Town?"

"Naw, it's too late for all that," Mase said.

"You sure?"

"The rain ain't coming down like before," Mase said, as an explanation. "The corner boys in Mexico Town have to be out now. They probably see us and figure us for easy targets."

Book again agreed.

"We'll just go around them," Mase said with a smile.

"Hey, Mase, I got a question," Book said as they walked down the darkened street.

"Go 'head," Mase said.

"You know po-po isn't that far from where Chocolate set up? Right?"

Mase listened.

"Well, I was wondering why he set up near the lock up spot?"

"Well, far as I can tell, Chocolate is a distributor. He ain't selling it near his spot. The sales are elsewhere," Mase said. He paused. "I think he wanted protection, in a strange way, from his enemies."

"That's crazy," Book said with a chuckle.

"It's no crazier than sending us almost up to 8 Mile to squash something between the two biggest kingpins and neither one of them telling us what we carrying," Mase said. "It's the game. We mules," Mase said, looking back to Book.

Book smirked and then agreed.

"We just got to get these backpacks to Chocolate and get paid," Mase eased up as he approached the corner. He reached out to Book and pointed to the corner and a group of corner boys on the opposite side of the street from a big box liquor store with a neon sign that read Shaun's Party Store.

Mase tapped Book and the two walked, then ran, in between the four open lots before the last house on Vinewood Street. The two ran and finding themselves in the alleyway only paused long enough to cut through a thick group of trees that stretched from the alleyway to the sidewalk of West Grand Boulevard.

On West Grand Boulevard Mase and Book moved as quickly as they could, running a block and walking a block at Porter Street as a bus pulled up to a bus stop. The boys ran on as Mase pointed out the freeway just ahead.

"This ain't a smart move," Mase said to himself more than to Book.

"Why?"

"Because everyone knows we're carrying," Mase said. "All someone has to do is roll up on us and our run is over."

"Naw, we close," Book said, reaching out and putting a hand on Mase's shoulder.

"Yeah, maybe you're right," Mase said.

The two boys walked on silently as the rain diminished and returned to its misting annoyance.

Mase kept looking back and Book looked back because of Mase.

"We need to get off this street," Mase said. "There's just too many eyes around," he added.

Book didn't respond.

Chapter 10.
West Grand Avenue

Book pointed out a driveway and Mase and he entered the driveway of an apartment complex off West Grand Avenue. The apartment complex had one of those electronic guard arms that stopped most cars and trucks, but not Mase or Book. The boys walked around the guard arms and into the parking lot and entrance to the nameless building. Mase and Book did not pay the building much attention as they walked trying to find a way to get to the freeway without having to walk down West Grand Avenue.

Mase looked back and found Book by his side. Book pointed to a low stone wall. The boys climbed over the wall and found themselves in a quiet neighborhood. The two boys looked at each other and shrugged their shoulders at the oddity of a secluded neighborhood just off West Grand Avenue.

The pair ran past two parked cars in a driveway and across a backyard where a dog was chained to a tree. Mase did not stop when the dog began barking. He just ran straight across the yard to the fence and clambered over with Book just a few steps behind. On the other side of the fencing there was another backyard, sans dog and house. Mase ran to where the house should have been and ran around a tree that had laid claim to the property.

On the other side of the tree was a picket fence that like the neighborhood was missing enough boards that it was more a frame than fence. Mase ducked under the framing of the fence and found himself and Book on West Lafayette Boulevard.

Without thought Mase pushed Book right and he and Book found themselves nearly back at Chocolate's distribution center.

"We need to get off this busy street?"

Mase looked at Book. He was learning. Busy streets were where corner boys liked to congregate, Mase tried to explain to everyone and anyone thinking about running product.

"The easiest way to get your packages jacked is walking or running on busy streets," Mase said looking for a side street.

Before he could find a side street Book reached out and grabbed his arm. Mase looked up and saw what made Book get his attention.

Three corner boys were walking toward them on their side of the street.

"Let's cross the street. If they follow, run down to Fisher and we can lose them down there," Mase said, looking at the oncoming traffic and back at the flow of traffic.

Book kept looking at the three corner boys walking toward them like they were out for a late-night stroll.

Mase stepped off the curb. Book did too.

"Hey, where you going, youngblood?"

Mase timed his next step perfectly. As a car whipped past Mase stepped into the lane and sidestepped into the next lane, putting himself halfway across the street.

Behind the three corner boys two others were suddenly scrambling to cross the street against the traffic.

Book was the first to make it safely across West Lafayette Boulevard with Mase seconds behind.

"Cut through one of those apartments," Mase said.

Book began to run. Mase ran as well. Behind the two boys ran the two corner boys who were brave enough the cross the avenue.

Book led the way to the rear of the apartment. Mase looked up and pointed to the walkway that stretched over Fisher Freeway. Book followed Mase's finger and began running toward the walkway.

The walkway gate was chained open and Book and Mase ran into the stairway and pounded up to the top with the three corner boys now in hot pursuit.

Mase and Book ran across the walkway and over the Fisher Freeway. At the end of the walkway, they jumped and bounded down the stairs to the other side.

They were suddenly on West Fisher Service Drive.

"Okay, I'm getting sick of this. Let's just get to Chocolate's," Mase said, suddenly frustrated.

Book laughed.

"What you laughing at?"

"You think just because you say it things are suddenly going to go our way?" Book asked.

"Why not?"

"Never happens that way," Book said.

Mase snickered. "Maybe you're right."

They were on the other side of the freeway. Mase looked and oriented himself with the area. The fifteen-year-old realized they were near Clark Street. They were just passing the brake shop and just ahead was a stop light that signaled Clark Street.

"Clark Street," Mase said with a smile. They were really close to Chocolate's secret hideout.

Book agreed.

They both knew that Southwest Detroit was a more industrial area on the side of the freeway they were on, but just on the other side of the freeway was the best Mexican food in Detroit. There were hole in the wall restaurants that made authentic Mexican meals that people lined up to eat. Yet, at that time of night the tourists, most of the tourists, were gone. In their place there were packs of renegades who loved to rob people, usually younger people, hoping to come up with a score of a drug mule or runner, like Mase and Book.

Mase checked his pockets and knew the only thing he had was a cell phone just in case things got hairy. Book too was only carrying a cell phone. They were runners. If they ran into any trouble they were supposed to run. They didn't need to be strapped. Any sign of trouble they were told always to slap their feet.

"You ready?"

Book assented.

"Okay," Mase said. "Same bet as before?"

Book nodded his agreement.

The second underpass race was won by Book. The underpass was also twice as long as the first one. It ran underneath Fisher Freeway. The two boys ran and halfway across the darkness Book seemed to find his stride. He took off. Mase tried to catch the faster boy. Book learned from the last race and instead of trying to run down the steps on the far side he jumped from the top and landed ahead of Mase.

Mase and Book laughed on the other side of the underpass.

"Even money," Book said.

Mase grinned.

Book looked up at the dark sky and the raindrops falling.

"Let's go," Book said.

Mase and Book cut across the lot and watched as the car which had been following them drove down a street a block from them. The pair froze and allowed the car to disappear before they crossed the street.

The pair started to run down Clark Street only to pause at the stop light before crossing. On the right was Clark Park sitting in the darkness. On the left was the corner store. In the darkness Mase noticed one of the shapes move. He reached out and touched Book, getting his attention.

"We might have trouble," Mase said.

Book looked in the direction Mase was gesturing.

Under the awnings of the building to protect them from the falling rain stood a couple of corner boys. Three broke from the shelter of the building and began crossing the street.

While Mase was focusing on the corner boys near the building he nearly ran into a smiling boy in front of him.

Chapter 11.
Cowboy up

"Howdy, boys," a tall, thin brown boy wearing a big cowboy hat said. He was brown and pimply faced, with a big nose and crooked teeth. He was wearing a two-piece rain suit in military green, Mase noted. On his feet were curled black cowboy boots.

Mase stopped short. Book instinctively stepped back, but the boy in the cowboy hat was not alone. There were three others with him. A big bald muscle-bound sepia hued thug wearing a rain slicker reached out and grabbed Book by his sweatshirt front. Beside the muscle-bound thug was a brownish boy wearing one of those yellow ponchos to keep the rain off, with a two-inch-tall Mohawk, wearing thick glasses and a sporting a nose ring. Closest to the boy in the cowboy hat was a pencil thin white girl holding a clear umbrella and wearing a transparent plastic get up to keep the rain off, underneath the plastic she showed off her pale white bony form dressed in a T-shirt which read: Lover. She wore booty shorts which highlighted her lack of a booty and yellow rubber boots.

"What brings you to our little bit of paradise?" The black cowboy asked Mase.

"Hey, get off me," Book said, trying to twist out of the grip of the bald muscle-bound thug. Mase turned to see what was going on and that was when the cowboy hit him in the side of the head. Mase did not go down. He had been turning and the blow had been glancing off his temple. He spun and found the skinny white girl clapping and bouncing up and down like she was watching a concert from the front row. Mase spun and threw an unaimed punch in the direction of the boy with the cowboy hat who was closing in on him.

Mase took a step forward and quite unexpectedly found his shiny, plastic backpack snatched off his back. He turned to see there were two others who had joined this motley crew. The dark boy holding his shiny, plastic yellow backpack in his hand had ears which stuck out from his V-shaped face. He had a nose ring and a stud earring. He was wearing a trench coat and hobnail boots. Mase noted on his wrist dangled what looked like a spiked dog collar. The last member of the jackers was a dark figure holding an umbrella and wearing a rain slicker. He was wearing jeans and sneakers.

Mase turned to the dark boy holding his yellow backpack.

"Give me that," Mase said, his voice in a growl.

"You think you bad enough to make me?" The cowboy asked, with a. crooked smile

Mase didn't answer. He looked back and the cowboy hat seemed happy to watch Mase against the boy with the big ears. Turning back big ears threw a punch and Mase dodged it.

The boy with the big ears snarled and looked like he was ready for a heads-up fight. Instead, Mase jumped and dived on the boy, who looked to be at least a few years older and easily thirty pounds heavier. Mase was in motion. In the rain and adrenalin charged action things sped up.

The boy seemed to be prepared for Mase's attack. He had dropped Mase's backpack and rolled with the attack. The two rolled in the street as Mase tried to free himself from beneath the heavier boy as quickly as he could and hit him in the face as many times as possible.

So many things happened in that moment. Mase tried to register everything. The boy in the cowboy hat stepped forward and reached out for the yellow backpack. The boy with the umbrella stood under the light of the streetlight overhead like some wannabe Charlie Chaplin and looked bored.

To the left of the fake Charlie Chaplin Book was in a tug-of-war with the musclebound thug. The boy in the yellow poncho kicked at Book and threw unaimed punches which seemed more for show than damage. In response, Book kicked at the boy and the boy stepped back behind the bigger thug. The skinny white girl grinned and showed off her crooked, yellow teeth and continued clapping. Somehow, she was near Book.

Mase focused on the boy he was wrestling with. The boy, who was bigger and heavier, was prepared as he could be for Mase's attack, but Mase was slippery. He was dripping wet. So, the boy could not get a good grip on him. Mase and the boy rolled to a stop. Mase got to his knees and fired several punches at the boy seeing the other boy with the umbrella jump back and away from him.

Instantly, Mase climbed to his feet and locating his shiny, plastic backpack ran to it. He turned and seeing Book running toward him ran in the same direction, away from the jackers.

When the pair turned away from the jackers and began to run they did not stop at the bottom of the street and were nearly hit by a car on West Fisher Service Drive. Book and Mase had to jump out of the path of the distracted driver. Mase then Book slammed into the side of a car parked in front of a dive bar and watched as the jackers came running after them. The pair ran two blocks before slowing down and looking back.

Mase and Book slowed their pace and stopped a little past Lansing Street. Mase had a cut over his left eye from the cowboy who had sucker punched him. He massaged his jaw where the boy with the big ears had hit him. Besides that, he was a little bruised but no real complaints.

"You, okay?"

"No," Book said. "That bitch had a knife. She stabbed me."

Mase looked at Book and checked to see where he had been stabbed. He was bleeding. The stab was more of a cut. He had been cut a few inches above his waistband on the left side.

"You'll be okay," Mase said, with a slight grin. "It's just a scratch."

"Don't feel like a scratch," Book said, frowning.

"You'll be fine," Mase said.

Book agreed.

After checking his wound Mase checked so see if Book still had his backpack. He did. The backpack was unzipped. Mase zipped it back up. He checked his shiny, plastic backpack as well. Unlike Book his backpack was undisturbed.

"Okay, let's get to Chocolate and drop this shit off," Mase said.

"Yeah, tonight is shit," Book said holding his side.

Book stood up and felt the twinge of pain from the recent stab wound he received from the crazy white girl. He pressed his hand against his side and looked at Mase and then the street they were on. Cars roared by on the freeway just a few feet away.

The pair of boys were near the corner of Ferdinand. There were half a dozen cars parked at the corner and Mase dragged Book along the dark street.

"It hurts," Book said, as he tried to will himself forward and not cry out in pain.

"Okay," Mase said looking for someplace to stop and check Book's wound. He saw that Ferdinand was empty of houses except at the top of the street. So, Mase walked Book to the closest streetlight and examined the wound Book was squeezing on his side.

Under the streetlight Mase lifted up Book's sweatshirt.

Book closed his eyes to the examination. The thirteen-year-old tried not to think about the girl with the crazy eyes laughing and stabbing him just a few minutes ago. His mind returned to how he had gotten to this point.

He had picked this life. He had decided this was going to be his get by until something better happened. Now, he was bleeding and trying to drop off a package and get out of his wet clothes.

Book was all of twelve going on thirteen when he dropped out of middle school, fed up with teachers, rules, classrooms and schedules. He had figured he would get into rap music or video games and when he realized neither option was a reality he turned to the streets.

He was kicked out of his mother's house and couch surfing when he met up with Mase. Mase and Book were play cousins. The two had gone to the same middle school before Mase transferred out. Mase had dropped out of school a few years later, but was making ends meet by working for Chocolate, one of downtown's big time drug dealers.

"How did you get in the game?" Book asked, curious.

"What you mean?" Mase asked. "I been pulled to this on and off for years."

"When did you decide...?" Book asked not knowing how to ask Mase his decision making to choose the street.

"Well, I was sort of fed-up with the whole school thing for as long as I can remember," Mase said. He shook his head at the thought. "I mean, it was cool and all learning about colors and numbers and stuff, but the rest didn't seem to matter."

"What?" Book asked.

"I mean, addition and subtraction make sense. That's money," Mase said. "Multiplying sort of makes sense but division and percentages don't mean shit to me or anyone I know. If they mark something down, I know that they marked it up in the first place. That was when I started to think that school wasn't for me."

"But, ain't you afraid?" Book asked, tentatively.

"Afraid of what?" Mase asked, unsure.

"Going to jail or...?" Book asked, trailing off. Again, not sure what to say.

"I ain't afraid to go to jail. We in jail right now, we just don't see the bars. We ain't free. Every day we walk around, and everyone is just waiting. They waiting to see if you live or if you get caught up in some bullshit and they kill you and blame you for dying." Mase laughed at the idea. "I mean, can you imagine that? We the only people brought here against our will and forced to work for them and they hate us for not dying. They hate us for not just giving up and becoming their dogs or pets." Mase looked at Book. Book listened quietly. Mase was angry. "We can't go everywhere. Everyone knows that. This place is fucked up from the front to the back. We here but we ain't really here." He paused.

"What you mean?" Book asked.

"We walking and talking and all the other shit, but we shadows, ghosts, and memories to them," Mase said, thoughtfully. "We remind them of all the wrong they committed. And that's the reason they want to kill us. They don't understand dying? My uncle, if he was my uncle, told me once that we, us, are dying every day, just a little bit at a time, from the moment we are born. Dying is going to happen. There's no Get Out of Dying card for anyone."

Chapter 12.
Criminal Thoughts

The physical examination did not take long, but Book recalled all the twists and turns being associated with Mase and The Hittas that had gotten him stabbed and bleeding on a side street. He shook his head thinking that he had at one time thought this life was full of money, adventure and glamour. The first few months were exciting. Book had made more money in a month than any grown up he knew.

"The way I see it we come into this world, and we don't have a say about it. I didn't ask to be born. I didn't ask to be black. I didn't ask for people to see me as a... criminal. But every day they look at me and judge me before I open my black mouth," Mase said. "My mom died. My grams, her mom, tried to raise me," Mase said with a shake of his head. "My dad, whoever he was, ghosted. My Grams is sick right now and I can't be around her. I can't sit and watch her... die."

Book, a few months after he turned thirteen, was introduced to... Chocolate Nathaniel. Well, a few months after he turned thirteen, Book was reintroduced to Mase, a school friend who pretended to be Book's cousin. Mase, fifteen and full of piss and vinegar, had stopped going to school a year after stepping into the local High School. He had argued with his grandmother for a week and by Friday decided he was done with school.

When Book showed up on the corner Mase was a little surprised.

"What you doing down here?" Mase asked.

"I'm done with all that nonsense they trying to teach me," Book said.

"All right, bet," Mase said. "The problem with all you schoolboys that get tired of school is that you ain't ready to get dirty. You like dressing up and playing bad. Down here, we ain't playing. We ain't got time for playing, especially when it comes to money."

"I get it," Book said.

"You get it?" Mase laughed.

"Well, if you get it, know that we are all trying to come up. Ain't nobody down here just because. They ain't worried about me. They want me to do the work," Mase said, explaining the street game. "The ones to watch are the ones near you. They are all haters unless you they blood."

Book had watched Mase and everything he did. He was a runner for Jesse, the corner boy who worked for Chocolate. Mase, after a week, introduced Book to Jesse.

Jesse was a skinny, jumpy teenager who looked like he could have worked at Best Buy. He had a friendly face, bushy eyebrows, smiling eyes and a big smile. He was sand colored and had a curly head of reddish-brown hair atop his oval head. Jesse liked to wear khakis instead of jeans and the Best Buy bright blue polo shirts for some reason. The whole Best Buy look worked in it threw off any suspicion Jesse was always armed and dangerous. The first thought about Jesse was he was just getting off from work. Not, he was working for Chocolate Nathaniel.

When Mase took Book to meet Jesse he was disciplining a spotter behind a warehouse. The spotter had gotten a little careless and nearly brought the po-po down on their corner. Two of his enforcers, thick armed brutes dressed in black hoodies, baggy jeans, and sneakers, were holding the spotter as Jesse kicked him repeatedly in the stomach.

"Everyone makes mistakes," Jesse said, catching his breath. He checked his shoes and hands to see if there was any blood on either. "Just understand," he said to the spotter laying on the ground behind the warehouse, with the big friendly smile. "When you working for me, you already got one strike. So, this fuck up is your second strike." Jesse pulled out his pistol from underneath his shirt. "You don't want to make a third strike with me." He paused. "Am I clear?"

The spotter grunted his answer, and the enforcers dragged him away. Mase and Book stood and waited. They did not talk. There wasn't much to say. Jesse turned and seeing Mase beckoned him over. Mase slowly closed the distance. Jesse still holding the pistol in his hand scowled awkwardly and slipped the hand cannon underneath his shirt.

Jesse and Mase dapped and nodded to each other. Jesse the booter disappeared, replaced with the Best Buy Jesse. The Best Buy Jesse, the friendly, unassuming character studied Book. Book stood in front of the boy who he had watched just seconds ago kick a boy mercilessly.

"Mase says that you ready to work," Jesse said.

Book agreed.

"You know these streets?" Jesse asked.

Book nodded silently again.

"Okay, take this package to Lowell Park. There's a guy that should be posted up at one of the chess tables. Ask for Shell. Give it only to Shell," Jesse said. He pulled out a manila envelope folded over and taped.

Book examined the envelope but did not move.

"Go nigguh," Jesse said.

Book shook his head, still holding the package in his hands.

"What nigguh?" Jesse asked with a frown.

"How will I know who this Shell is?" Book asked.

Jesse smirked. He looked at Mase and grinned showing off his gold grill.

"He is this blue black nigguh. I mean, ink black. He should be wearing a Raiders sweatshirt or Raider hat for some reason. That nigguh loves the Raiders. I can't explain that," Jesse said with a shake of his head. He looked at Book, questioningly. "Anything else, little nigguh?"

"Naw," Book said. "Lowell Park. Blue black Shell. Raiders' sweatshirt. Got it."

Book slipped the package Jesse gave him into his jacket and disappeared.

Mase looked at Jesse and laughed. As the two watched Book run away from them Mase looked at Jesse. Jesse sneered.

"Is Shell there?" Mase asked.

"He should be," Jesse said. "He working for me."

About an hour later Book returned and told Jesse he had given the package to Shell.

Jesse looked at Book confused.

"How I know you didn't take my shit, little nigguh?" Jesse asked.

Jesse pulled his pistol and stepped menacingly toward Book.

Book raised his hands and in one was his cell phone.

"I took a picture," Book said. "I told Shell that once you saw the picture, I would delete it."

Book handed Jesse his phone and there on the screen was Book and a skeletal black brother with big lips and ears wearing an Oakland Raiders' sweatshirt and looking at the screen, next to Book. Shell had the package in his hand.

Jesse slipped his gun back under his shirt and tossed Book back his phone.

"I like you Book," Jesse said. "I like a smart little nigguh."

"How much I get for that run?" Book asked.

"How much?" Jesse asked, with a smile. "I figure a good runner gets good money. Say twenty a run?"

"The spotters offered me that," Book said with a chuckle. "You bigger than them? You running things. I say a hundred a run," Book said. "That's cheap. No one knows me. I'm invisible."

"A Franklin?" Jesse said, looking at Book through his hard, dark eyes. "You keep track of the runs and if you don't fuck up and I don't murk you then I'll pay you."

"Every day I do a run?" Book asked.

"Yeah, little nigguh, every day you do a run," Jesse said, with a scowl.

Jesse tested out Book the rest of the day. The corner boy had him run a few things for him. Every time Book returned, and Jesse threatened him as if he was going to shoot him. Then he did not shoot him. A day turned into a week. A week turned into a month.

Mase watched from afar. Mase heard good things about Book. Sonny heard good things about Book as well. Sonny and Mase talked. After a month of not fucking up Jesse introduced Book to Sonny, the juice on the street.

Sonny was a dangerous high-strung type. He was always strapped and tended to shoot first and ask questions later. He was a sand-colored man with wavy black hair and intense eyes. Around his neck was a thick gold chain with the gold and diamonds Hitta medallion dangling from it. He liked to dress in sweats most of the time. Occasionally he wore jeans, but more often Sonny was found in his designer sweats.

Mase was there when Sonny met Book. They were in a mall parking lot for some reason. There were dozens of people walking in and out of the mall stores. Sonny was in the back of the Lexus RX waiting for someone to show up when Book appeared with Mase. Mase was his validation.

"Hear good things about you," Sonny said watching everyone and everything around him.

Book did not comment.

"You ready to work with someone with weight?" Sonny asked.

"Yep," Book said. Mase had laughed.

"You know working with me ain't no game," Sonny said, as a warning.

Book lowered his eyes only to look up.

"He don't say much," Sonny said to Mase.

"He more a thinker than a talker," Mase said.

Book didn't disagree.

"All right, little nigguh," Sonny said, with a smirk. "I'll try you out. If you don't fuck up, then we keep going." The weight of the street said. "You good with that?"

"How much per run?" Book asked.

Sonny smirked. "I like that. You all business. Me too." Sonny studied Book. "How much Jesse giving you?"

"A hundred a run," Book said.

"If you don't fuck up and I don't kill you myself I'll double that," Sonny said. "That good?"

Book allowed a slight grin to appear on his face.

Book shadowed Sonny that first week and did half a dozen runs without problem. The second week Book was running everywhere. He would drop off one package and when he returned Sonny had another package ready to go. Book never complained.

After three weeks, Book was asked to take a package to the Newark Street Graffiti Wall to a corner boy named Zeus. The run was just four blocks over from where Sonny was at the time. Sonny gave him the package and Book ran to the spot looking for Zeus. The corner boys said there was no Zeus there. Book knew something was wrong. The corner boys tried to rob Book. Book beat his feet and outran the corner boys.

He returned to Sonny with the package and told him exactly what had happened. Mase was there as Book gave Sonny the blow-by-blow details. He did not leave anything out.

"You know, we need little nigguhs like you Book," Sonny said with a smile.

Later, Book and Mase talked.

"What was that all about?" Mase asked.

"Think some of the corner boys aren't happy with Sonny, for some reason," Book said. "Hear things when I'm delivering. Don't say anything. Just listen."

"Think it's bad for Sonny?" Mase asked.

"Not sure," Book said. "Streets is always talking about one thing or another."

Sonny wanted to take Book under his wing, but before the next month Sonny was dead. He had been in a shootout and lost.

It had been just a week after Sonny was put in the ground Mase delivered Book to Chocolate. Because Mase had vouched for Book he was sort of attached to the thirteen-year-old. When Chocolate sent for Book, he made sure Mase was there as well. Book was nearly four months in the Hittas game when he and Mase met with Chocolate.

Chapter 13.
Elevenish

The three sat in the small and dimly lit local bar and drank their beers and talked and laughed as the others in the bar watched them cautiously. Keyon, the biggest of the three, sat and scanned the interior of the bar. When they entered there were no more than ten people in the bar including the bartender and barmaid. At the bar sat four men, all in their late fifties, potbellied, out of shape and drinking draft beer or whiskey. At the five tables around Keyon, Jayson and Gerald were four other men who seemed grouped in pairs and maybe dock workers taking a break or on their way home, dressed in coveralls, work boots and heavy jackets. There were two lone drinkers.

Gerald watched Keyon watching the bar. He knew his military minded friend was scoping out the bar for any threats. There was a slight tension in the bar, initially, but it abated, just enough for Keyon to relax.

"You know we're not in Fallujah?"

"Yeah, I know, but sometimes it sort of feels like we are," Keyon said, looking at his drink in front of him. He twirled the glass around in his hand.

"You need to relax," Gerald said, looking at Keyon with a slight grin. He turned and looked for Jayson. "You need to be more like Jay."

Gerald tipped his head in the direction of Jayson. Keyon followed Gerald's gesture. Jayson seemed oblivious to the tension. He was focused on the three slot machines hiding in the rear of the bar. He was seated in front of one of the machines and feeding it quarters.

"What? That boy needs to call Gamblers Anonymous," Keyon said, with a chuckle.

Gerald shook his head at the comment. In front of him was his Zombie Dust beer. He had been nursing it since the trio arrived.

"How's that beer?"

"It's definitely different," Gerald said, sticking out his lower lip. "It's not bad at all."

"Yeah, you keep telling yourself that," Keyon said with a smile.

The two sat at the table and listened to the hits from 50's playing on the jukebox.

"You know I'm going to find a decent song on that jukebox," Keyon said throwing back his second tequila shot. He climbed to his feet and walked to the jukebox. Gerald watched as Keyon arrived at the old-fashioned jukebox and studied the selections. Gerald could only chuckle at Keyon stuck in front of the jukebox, trying to find a "decent song" in the box.

Keyon returned to the table with a big smile on his face.

"You find something?" Gerald asked.

"I did," Keyon said smugly.

Gerald lifted his beer and checked how much remained.

"Well, when I finish this, we're heading out," Gerald said to Keyon.

"I thought you didn't have to work tomorrow?" Keyon asked.

"I didn't say that," Gerald said. "I said that I don't have kids in the classroom tomorrow," he said, correcting Keyon.

Keyon looked at Gerald confused.

"I can't stay out all night Key," Gerald said, looking at the big goof in front of him.

"Well, we have to stay until I hear my song," Keyon said. He added, "That's only fair."

"Yeah, that's only fair." Gerald said.

Gerald sipped his beer and Keyon ordered a Bell's Two Hearted Ale from right here in Michigan by way of Seattle as his last drink.

"Jay? You want anything else?" Keyon asked.

"I'll have what you're having," Jayson said from the corner of the bar.

Keyon ordered a Bell's Two Hearted Ale for Jayson and the pair sat and drank their beers and waited for Keyon's song to play.

Gerald was nearly finished drinking his beer and Jayson was halfway through his when the classic keyboard and harmonica sound pierced the night and interior of Face Down. Keyon blinked. Jayson blinked and grinned as well from the corner.

"This is your song?" Gerald asked.

"Yeah, I didn't have a bunch of choices," Keyon said.

"Nice choice," Gerald said.

The bar was bathed in the 1973 classic hit by Stevie Wonder. The bar fell away as the blind musician sang of believing in things you don't understand. None of the three had been alive when Stevie Wonder penned the classic, but they knew the song. Everyone knew the song. For the three minutes Stevie Wonder sang and played Face Down was transported, transformed and everyone was back in 1973.

"All right, I'm calling it a night," Gerald said, checking his wristwatch. It was nearly eleven o'clock. "And because I'm driving that means you two are calling it a night too."

Jayson, the newly hired, threw up a finger and grabbed his beer. He chugged it down to the broadening smile of Keyon and Gerald. On the table was a paper bucket of quarters Jayson had won.

"Always the beer hound," Keyon said with a shake of his head.

"How much you win?" Gerald asked.

"Shit, man, I think I came away with forty or fifty dollars tonight," Jayson said. "Not a bad night."

Gerald waved to the bartender behind the bar and headed to the exit. He paused seeing the rain just beginning to intensify. Behind him followed Jayson and Keyon.

"Luckily, we aren't that far," Gerald said. He looked back at Jayson and Keyon who made faces seeing the rain falling just on the other side of the door to the bar.

"Run," Gerald said and instantly he was in motion. He high stepped across the sidewalk and into the street just enough to run along the side of the street closest to the cars. He ran past two then three cars parked near the bar and skidded to a stop. On the sidewalk, Keyon and Jayson were fighting to be the first to the car. Neither had a jacket or umbrella.

Jayson was near the car when he spilled some quarters. He turned around and looked for the suddenly invisible coins in the dark and rain. Keyon laughed and ran past Jayson.

"Come on cheapskate," Keyon said with a laugh.

Jayson reluctantly turned and followed Keyon.

Gerald ran to his car and skidding to the driver's side door, kicked a hefty bundle near his back wheel. The bundle slid forward and lodged under the front wheel. Gerald unlocked the car. He opened the car and was about to climb in when he looked down. In the interior light of the car Gerald could just make out the green and black writing underneath a tightly wrapped plastic. The bundle was easily thicker than a brick. Gerald climbed into the car and out of the rain and found himself unable to close the car door despite the rain. He looked down, at the bundle just inches from his car door.

Gerald blinked, thinking he was seeing things. He looked again. There was a stack of bills in a plastic wrapping just under his doorframe. Gerald closed his eyes again and opened them again, after a quick silent prayer. There, just in arm's reach rested a stack of bills. He looked left and right. He picked it up. It was hefty and two bricks wide. There was a real weight to the money and for some reason Gerald could not believe his luck. He closed the car door and placed the bundle on his lap. Gerald looked down at the familiar face of Benjamin Franklin looking back at him underneath the plastic. Gerald sat in the car, bewildered.

Keyon, sitting in the passenger seat, saw Gerald with the bundle in his hand and then on his lap.

"What is that?" Gerald sat under the steering wheel holding what must be hundreds if not thousands of hundred-dollar bills.

Jayson climbed into the back of the BMW. He was dripping wet and cradling his small beaten-up paper bucket of quarters.

"Man, it's raining cats and dogs," Jayson said, wiping the rain from his face and noticing Gerald and Keyon silent in the car. He investigated and saw Gerald holding the huge plastic bundle of cash.

"Where in the fuck did you get that?" Jayson asked.

"It was outside my car door," Gerald said.

"Damn," Jayson said. He leaned forward to get a better look at the stack of money.

"What you thinking?" Keyon asked.

"You think it's stolen?" Asked Jayson.

Gerald smiled and Keyon shook his head at Jayson.

"What's the plan?" Keyon asked Gerald.

"Think it's fake?" Jayson asked.

"Fake? Why would you think that?" Keyon asked.

"Don't nobody lose that kind of money and not come back and get it," Jayson said.

"Gee? What's the plan?" Keyon said, dismissing Jayson.

"What do you mean? It ain't *our* money," Jayson said.

"It ain't *our* money, is right," Gerald said to Keyon.

"You going to be like that?" Keyon asked looking at Gerald.

"What do you mean like that?" Gerald asked.

"Stingy," Keyon said.

"Stingy? How is it stingy when I found this?" Gerald asked.

"You wouldn't have found it if it wasn't for us," Keyon said.

"What if I had found a bag of shit? Would you want me to split that?" Gerald asked.

"Hell, no," Keyon said.

Gerald smiled.

"We all benefit from a little cash flow," Jayson said from the back of the BMW.

"You got a plan?" Keyon asked studying Gerald.

"I'm not sure," Gerald said. He knew he was talking, listening, and trying to take in all the information, but it all was coming in too fast.

"Okay, the first thing we need to do is shake the spot," Keyon said.

"Yeah, if someone is looking for this bundle, then we shouldn't be here when they come looking," Jayson said.

"Okay," Gerald said, starting the car and slowly sitting the bundle on the armrest between him and Keyon.

"What? You all of a sudden don't trust us?" Keyon asked, looking at Gerald.

"Naw, it ain't like that," Gerald said with a smile. He reached out and handed the bundle to Keyon.

"All right," Keyon said with a smile.

Gerald shook his head as they drove away from the bar and toward downtown.

"Finder's keepers, loser's weepers," said Jayson from the rear of the BMW.

Chapter 14.
Chocolate Nathaniel

Now everyone in Southwest Detroit knew Chocolate Nathaniel. Before he was the biggest dope dealers downtown, he was Nathaniel Ocean, the son of Suzanne Ocean. The Oceans lived near Clark Park. Chocolate had gone to high school at Western International High School and played basketball there for a year before dropping out and starting his street career. He was a cold-hearted individual who was always interested in money over everything. Nathaniel rose up through the ranks of the Hittas and by the time he was nineteen he was a trusted lieutenant for the head of the Hittas.

The Hittas, before Chocolate took over, were run by a psychotic leader called on the street: Deadeye Von. Under Von were the three friends he had grown up with, Clay, Ennis, and Hasan. Ocean worked for Ennis.

There was a falling out between Von and his friends. One thing led to another and one night Von, Clay and Hasan were dead. The lieutenants underneath attacked and killed Ennis.

Chocolate took his revenge on the surviving lieutenants and at twenty-three took control of the Hittas. He had been in control of the gang for nearly four years, which on the street was like twenty years. Chocolate had squashed all beefs after the murders of Von and his three power hungry friends. The Hittas shutdown all squabbles and focused on money and power. So, when Book and Mase met with Chocolate it was a big deal.

Chocolate was the top of the Hittas. Meeting up with Chocolate was the biggest deal for anyone in the Hittas. Mase and Book, with hopes that he might tag one or both as a regular runner, was a big deal for the teenagers.

For Mase, meeting with Chocolate was like meeting royalty. He liked it and couldn't deny that he was hoping the leader of the

Hittas would consider him as a personal runner. Chocolate's personal runners made bank. Mase made two bills a run. Book was making a hundred a run and hoping to move up the line.

The meeting with Chocolate Nathaniel was in the bleachers at Clark Park. There was a little league baseball game going on when Book and Mase showed up. The pair were stopped by the first level of security, a hard guy wearing a hooded sweatshirt, baggy jeans, and basketball sneakers.

"Who you looking for?"

Book didn't speak. Mase looked at the hard guy with his hand behind his back.

"We supposed to meet with Chocolate," Mase said. "Tell him it's Mase and Book."

The hard guy, with his hand behind his back, tapped his phone and said, "Two nigguhs for Chocolate. Mase and Book?"

Book looked at Mase. Mase stood and waited as women and children walked past them.

"Send 'em up," someone said on the phone and the hard guy tipped his chin in the direction of the snack shack. The pair walked in between the backstop and the snack shack and ran into the second level of security. Two men dressed in baggy jeans, basketball sneakers and hooded sweatshirts looked at Book and Mase.

The smaller of the two men with French braids and a thin mustache stuck out a hand.

"Either one of you heavy?"

Book looked and Mase and Mase and Book shook their heads.

The smaller thug stepped forward and frisked them. Both Mase and Book noticed both men were armed.

"Go on," the man with French braids said.

Chocolate Nathaniel was as small brown man who looked like he was not twenty-five. He had a V-shaped face, thin eyebrows, broad nose, and full lips. He was dressed in a sweatsuit, sneakers, and sunglasses. His black hair was braided and tight. Chocolate had a knife scar across his pointy chin.

"I hear good things about you," Chocolate Nathaniel said. In his ear was a diamond stud. On his wrist was an expensive gold wristwatch. Around his neck was a thick gold chain with a diamond encrusted letter H.

"You know my boy wanted you to sit up under him and learn the game before he got caught up?" Chocolate asked Book. Chocolate spoke watching everything. His eyes were hidden behind his reflective sunglasses.

Book and Mase listened. Mase sat by his play cousin.

"That is some high praise," Chocolate said. "How old are you?"

"Thirteen," Book said.

"That's a good age," Chocolate said. "You?"

Book looked at Chocolate and then Mase.

"Book," the teenager said.

"That's interesting. Okay, Book," Chocolate said with a grin.

Book stood silently. Mase listened.

"I'm going to give you a trial run," Chocolate said. "I left something in my office, and I need you to go get it."

Book perked up with the task. Then he frowned.

"What is it?" Chocolate asked.

"I ain't never been to your office," Book said. "I can't imagine anyone that works for you is going to let me in, in the first place, and more importantly, let me get something you need."

Chocolate laughed. "I like you," Chocolate said with a nod. "They said you were quick."

He was given a low-level job for Chocolate himself. He worked at the Amicci's Pizza spot watching for any unusual activity around one of Chocolate's bases. He was given a cellphone to call in any issues to one of two men watching over the complex. In all the time he worked for Chocolate he never had been in the complex.

Chocolate had allowed Book to work for him because Mase vouched for him.

"You fuck up and you fuck up my rep," Mase explained.

Book remembered the first time he was paid after meeting with Chocolate. The tall and dapper black man with a U-shaped face, big, friendly, and welcoming smile, dark eyes, broad nose, and thick eyebrows just appeared. He climbed out of a Cadillac Escalade driven by a dark giant. Delmar was dressed, the first time Book met him, in a white collared shirt, blueprint tie, black trousers and black lace-up boots. The man looked like he had come from a wedding or a funeral. In his earlobe was a golden star.

"You Book?"

Book nodded.

"I'm Delmar," the stranger said with a smile. "I'm the guy to pay you. If you have a problem on these streets, come to me. I handle it all." He paused and stepped closer to Book. Book instinctively took a step back.

Delmar sneered at Book's reticence.

"Remember, little nigguh, I'm the money man," Delmar said.

Book listened.

"If shit goes sideways out here, you tell me. I straighten things out," Delmar said.

Book nodded his head.

"I'll swing by and straighten you out each night. If you stepping off the spot early then come and see me at the ice cream shop, just down the way," Delmar said, hitching his thumb over his shoulder.

Book did not say anything.

Delmar grinned.

"You don't talk too much?"

Book looked at Delmar and tried to figure out the strange man in front of him.

"Well, little nigguh, I'm good," Delmar said, turning and starting to walk back to the Cadillac.

"Wait," Book said.

Delmar stopped and turned around with a smile.

"Where's my money?" Book asked.

Delmar smiled smugly. He tilted his head to the left and then to the right, looking at Book like he was looking for something hidden in his face. Book stood and waited.

"How much I owe you?" Delmar asked.

"Did four runs," Book said.

"That's six Benjamins?"

"Naw, that's eight Benjamins," Book said, correcting Delmar.

"I get a taste of your money to make sure you get your money," Delmar said.

Book laughed.

"Why you laughing?" Delmar asked.

"I know nigguhs like you," Book said. *"I made a deal with the boss. You feel good taking a taste of my cheddar? Then I'm going to feel good telling Chocolate that you skimming my cheddar."*

Delmar's smile evaporated with Book's words. He again looked at Book and tilted his head to the left and then the right. He paused and for a beat Delmar stood there thinking.

Book waited.

"I like you," Delmar said, with a smile.

Book got his money that night and every night following. There was no discrepancies. There were no issues.

Delmar was strange. He was dangerous. Yet, it was Delmar who paid Book. He was the man to collect his money regularly. Book became comfortable with the unpredictable Delmar because he saw the odd gangster so often.

Chapter 15.
Nearly Eleven thirty

Delmar and Pancake were sitting in the GLB when Mase and Book appeared at the corner of Porter and Lansing. The pair of boys inched toward the veterans as they moved slowly toward the complex Pancake pointed out the "little one" looked hurt. They sat in the Mercedes as Mase and Book got to the complex. Delmar was the first out of the SUV.

"What the fuck happened to you?" Delmar asked annoyed.

"We got jumped getting back here," Mase said, wiping the rain from his face and checking on Book.

Book winced, holding his side.

Delmar looked at Book. Pancake stood towering over all three.

"What happened to him?"

"He got cut," Mase said.

"Stabbed," Book said and winced, trying to stand in front of the two veterans.

"You got the backpacks?" Delmar asked, looking to see if they were still carrying the backpacks. He turned on his heels and led the pair to the rear of the house furthest from the corner. Mase and Book followed. Pancake brought up the rear.

They passed the two guards and entered the living room. Once inside the living room Mase and Book looked even more pathetic, all wet and bedraggled. Book was still bleeding and holding his side as the four climbed up the stairs to the second floor.

"Hey, do any of you got a first aid kit?" Delmar asked.

The two guards looked at Delmar and then at Book and Mase and shook their heads in response.

The four walked upstairs and into the boiler room and like the last time they had visited it was a hive of activity. There were people chopping, packing, weighing, and watching each other in the front of

"

the office. Two guards watched as Delmar led Book and Mase into the boiler room and to the rear of the second floor to Chocolate's office.

Delmar and Mase and Book walked past all of the activity with Pancake taking up the rear.

At Chocolate's door this time Delmar knocked. Delmar checked Book and Mase. Mase was wiping rainwater from his face. Book was holding his side. Pancake ambled up, not in a hurry.

"Come in," Chocolate said on the other side of the door.

After a beat Delmar walked in with the runners behind him.

"Boss, we had a little trouble," Delmar said.

Chocolate was sitting behind his desk. Next to him was this woman that could have been a model. She had long legs, arms, and fingers. Her hair was combed into a short Afro, and she was dressed in a basketball jersey, tight blue jeans, and basketball sneakers.

"Sit over there baby, while I take care of this," Chocolate said.

The girl pouted at Chocolate's words. She climbed off his lap and reluctantly separated from Chocolate but not before she gave him a kiss on the lips. The nameless girl moved slowly and deliberately to the overstuffed leather couch showing anyone and everyone who had eyes some incredible side boob. The nameless girl sat and picked up a magazine and began flipping through the pages.

"So, what is the trouble, Del?" Chocolate Nathaniel asked.

"Our little runner got nicked," Delmar said, pulling Book forward. Book winced with the effort.

Chocolate looked at Book and saw he was holding his side. Blood was dripping from where he clutched his side.

"Check the merchandise, then get him patched up," Chocolate said. He looked at Delmar evenly. "There should be six packs and two new hard to find boxes of Satan Shoes." Chocolate paused. "Take them out of here and drop my shoes at the door."

Delmar spun around and grabbed Book and pushed Mase toward the exit. Pancake was circling around the trio and unzipping the backpacks and pulling out the two shoe boxes. Pancake deposited the shoe boxes at the door as the four left Chocolate's office.

On the other side of the office door Delmar and Pancake pulled the bundles of cash from the backpacks. Delmar had two plastic bundles in his hands. Pancake had three.

"Turn around little nigguhs," Delmar said, his voice a hiss.

Mase and Book turned around.

"What the fuck?" Delmar said, annoyed.

Mase and Book looked silently.

"Where's the other stack?" Delmar asked.

Mase and Book looked at Delmar and then at each other uncomprehendingly.

"We light a stack," Delmar said, his voice growling.

"Well, maybe when we were jumped, we might have lost something," Mase said, guiltily.

"What the fuck you talking about?" Delmar asked, visibly upset.

"I told you we were jumped on the way back," Mase said, looking at Delmar.

"Yeah," Delmar said.

"Well, the only time our backpacks were off our backs was when they tried to jack us," Mase said, with a slight shrug of his shoulders.

"Hold up," Delmar said, looking at Mase seriously. "You saying that those jackers hijacked Chocolate's payment?"

"They the only ones that snatched our backpacks," Mase said. Book agreed.

"You know where you were jumped?" Delmar asked.

Mase bobbed his head. Book watched and bobbed his head too.

"Okay, you two stay here," Delmar said tapping the office door they were still in front of. He opened the door and Pancake and Delmar entered.

"What you think going to happen?" Book asked.

"Well, we ain't fucked up before," Mase admitted. "So, they might beat us up a bit but that'll be about all," Mase said.

"I seen them beat up people before. It ain't pretty." Book said.

"Yeah, they do it to keep us in line," Mase said. "We just be quiet and listen and learn."

A few minutes later Delmar and Pancake stepped out of the office.

"Chocolate ain't happy. He wanted to leak you both, but I told him you know where the jackers are and if we get the cheese back, he ain't going to be mad," Delmar said to Mase and Book.

The two boys listened and did not speak.

"Say something," Delmar said.

"Thanks," Mase said.

"Yeah, thanks," Book said.

"So, now, you and me going on a little ride to find our cheese," Delmar said to Mase and Book. "You better not be fucking with us. We don't like runners fucking with us."

Before leaving Pancake, the giant, checked Book's cut. He cleaned it up and patched him.

"If it's me, I go to the Emergency Room and get some stitches," Delmar said.

Book shook his head.

"Suit yourself," Delmar said. "I think before they had stitches nigguhs just bled until it stopped."

In the Mercedes Benz Delmar drove. Mase was in the passenger seat. Pancake sat in the rear with Book.

"Okay, tell me where to go," Delmar said, impatiently. "I don't want to be out here all night."

Mase gave him directions and Delmar headed down West Fisher Service Drive toward Clark Street. At the corner of Clark Street and West Fisher Service Drive Delmar turned the SUV left and drove slowly looking for the jackers.

Book reached up and tapped Mase.

The SUV slid past Face Down. The small bar seemed closed to all in the SUV. The only thing that suggested it was possibly open was the neon light which flickered in the front window.

"Yeah, yeah," Mase said. "Slow down," Mase said. "I think we were trying to cross Fisher when we got jumped," he added.

"I think so," Book said from the rear seat, next to Pancake.

"Should I stop? Delmar asked.

"No. I mean, yeah. This is it," Mase said.

Delmar pressed the brakes of the SUV but did not stop the car. It was library quiet.

"You said they jumped you by the park?"

Mase and Book nodded.

"We just passed where we got jumped," Mase said.

"Calm down, little nigguh," Delmar said with a smile. "I'm checking out the lay of the land. I don't want to turn off my car in the middle of a shootout."

Delmar drove the SUV to Porter Street and turned left and then made another left turn into a driveway of a house on the near empty block. He reversed the Mercedes and headed back to Clark Street.

"Can I ask a question?" Mase asked.

"Sure," Delmar said, looking at Mase as he pulled up to the corner of Porter Street and Clark Street.

"Why did Chocolate send us to Happy's?" Mase asked, looking at the dangerous Delmar.

"Shit if I know. Think they been at it for a while," Delmar said, pausing. He looked at Mase and smiled. "Way I hear it they were boys once. They might have gone to the same school for all I know. One thing led to another, and they had some kind of falling out. But they still kind of friends, in some kind of way. Shit is twisted. The package you took was supposed to be some kind of smoothing shit over kind of present for Happy."

"A present?" Mase asked, with a shake of his head.

"Yeah, that's all I got," Delmar said.

"Then why were they after us?" Mase asked.

Delmar smiled knowingly as he turned onto Clark Street. "I just learned this word from watching the news this week. Plausible denial." He smiled, full of himself. "You know what that mean?"

"Nope," Mase said.

"It means they could have murked you, jacked you and after it was all said and done said they didn't know shit about it," Delmar said with an evil grin on his face.

"They don't want things smoothed over?" Mase asked.

"Shit if I know," Delmar said. "I don't worry about shit that don't effect me."

Delmar pushed the brakes of the Mercedes GLB and parked a couple of hundred feet away from the food store. He left the car running. He looked at Mase and frowned. Mase noticed the frown this time was not the one that suggested that he wanted to beat his brains in, then and there.

"So, what you planning on doing?" Mase asked. "You find the jackers and make them give you back the money?"

"Yeah, that's the plan," Delmar said.

The Mercedes rolled down the street. Delmar looked at Mase and frowned.

"Were they corner boys?" Delmar asked.

"I think so," Mase said. He quickly added, "They had a white girl with them."

Delmar stopped the Mercedes in the middle of the street. He looked at Mase like he wanted to beat him then and there.

"You got anything else you forgot to tell me?" Delmar asked.

Mase shook his head in response.

"I told you little nigguh, I ain't got patience for this kind of shit," Delmar said, turning around under the steering wheel. He studied Mase intently. "I'm one second from whooping your ass on GP."

"That's it," Mase said.

"Okay, so we looking for some snow bunny slumming down here?" Delmar asked.

Mase nodded.

"Okay, this is the plan," Delmar said. "I'm leaving the car running in case shit goes south. Don't think shit's going south with a bunch of corner boys." He paused. "How many were there?"

"Six," Mase said. "And the girl."

"I'm going to go check the spot," Delmar said calmly. "If no one is around, we'll walk around and find these fucks. If they are there, then I'll talk to them and get our money back."

Delmar opened his car door and stepped out. Once outside of the SUV Delmar talked directly to Pancake.

"Pan, hold it down," Delmar said with a smile. "Don't let no one sneak up on me. If shit goes sideways, then come in wrecking shit." He paused and looked down the street.

Pancake nodded, placing a gigantic paw on the headrest of the Mercedes. Mase looked at the deep brown hand of Pancake and knew that it was nearly four times the size of his fifteen-year-old hand. He had once asked to measure his hand to Pancake's and been impressed with the sheer mass of the gangster.

Pancake had gotten his name from his ability to knock grown men on their back with little effort. He had been in a fight once and pancaked three men before getting shot. He had been shot, stabbed, and hit by a car and survived it all.

Pancake was this durable and brooding giant with a small box shaped head. He had a trimmed short Afro above his Neanderthal forehead and dull brown eyes. He had broken his nose so many times it had a strange unnatural bend to it which reminded many of his street nickname. The smashed nose sat above his trimmed mustache and goatee. He was three hundred pounds, at least, maybe six foot three or four with ham-sized mitts. He wore no jewelry. No watch, no rings, or earrings.

Chapter 16.
The bundle

Gerald drove away from Face Down silently. The Southwest Detroit lights, houses, buildings, and streets whipped by, but he barely noticed. In the car were Keyon and Jayson and a plastic bundle of cash. It was wide and heavy. Gerald tried to wrap his head around his luck.

"You think this is real?" Gerald asked, looking at the bundle.

Gerald looked out of the corner of his eye at the thick bundle of bills wrapped in unclouded plastic that could have been plastic wrap from someone's kitchen. The bills were stacked four across and about three inches thick.

"Not sure," Jayson said reaching for the bundle and Keyon handing it to him.

Gerald drove toward downtown. The music played in the car, but no one sang or seemed too focused on the selection.

"Did you see anyone when we left?" Keyon asked.

Jayson looked back to see if there were any cars following.

"No one's following us," Jayson said.

"How you know?" Gerald asked, looking at the rearview mirror and Jayson in the rear of the M3.

"There aren't any cars following us," Jayson said turning back and looking behind.

"If someone's following us, they ain't going to be on our bumper," Keyon said.

"Well, ain't no one following us right now," Jayson said.

Gerald drove not sure what to say. His mind was reeling. He tried to remain calm and cool in front of his friends, but inside he was screaming.

"If this is real money then things are about to change significantly," he thought. *"Why wouldn't it be real? No one was printing fake money in the Southwest. They didn't have the time or*

energy to do the long play. Everyone in Southwest Detroit was scrambling, like everyone in Detroit, in general, and trying to come up." Gerald tried to concentrate. Keyon and Jayson were trying to help but at the same time every word they spoke made Gerald want to pull over and kick them out. He needed to think, but that opportunity was gone now.

"You think it is one of those bank packets with an ink bomb inside?" Jayson asked.

"Why would you think that?" Keyon asked.

"What do you mean? It ain't normal to find a bundle of money at night," Jayson said. "So, I was trying to figure out where it came from. That makes sense."

"I don't think it's one of those bank ink bomb packets," Keyon said, lifting the bundle up. "Check it out. Whoever wrapped this wasn't a professional."

"How you know what a professional would do with stacks of money?" Jayson asked, skeptically.

Keyon shook his head.

"You know I work with professionals dealing with all sorts of cash," Keyon said.

Gerald listened to the conversation and suddenly had no words to offer. He was tasked with driving and that seemed to take up all of his energy.

"You think it's counterfeit?" Jayson asked.

"Well, if it ain't real it would be counterfeit, Jay," Keyon said, becoming pensive.

"It don't look fake," Jayson said.

"Now, if this is counterfeit then this might be some other level shit," Keyon said, serious. "Counterfeiters are no joke."

"Yeah, I don't think we're dealing with counterfeiters," Jayson said.

"I hope not," Keyon said from the front seat. "Counterfeiters and drug dealers are next level. Either of them would hunt us down. They are trouble."

"How you know so much about --" Jayson began and stopped himself.

"We all have to take a class on counterfeiting at the cannabis shop," Keyon said. "Counterfeiters are a problem. They are constantly trying to fool banks and retailers. So, when we opened, we had to learn all there was about these dickheads."

"I don't think this is fake money," Jayson said from the rear of the M3, holding the bundle.

"Why you say that?" Keyon asked.

"This is a whole lot of cheddar," Jayson said. "I ain't no funny money expert or nothing, but we ain't the ones that would have a bundle of funny money to lose," Jayson said, handing the stack back to Keyon. "That's a white boy game."

"If it's real then it is bad news," Keyon said, examining in the money as the car slid down the street back toward the Renaissance Center.

Gerald listened, caught up in his thoughts. He feathered the brakes of the M3 at the stop light and tried to remain calm. The light changed and he turned left and parked near the River Walk.

Gerald pulled the M3 over. The three sat in the plush interior of the M3 silent as church mice. The interior lighting dimmed. Gerald, Keyon, and Jayson just sat there looking at the plastic bundle.

"What do you think we should do?" Jayson asked, straight faced.

Everyone in the BMW laughed.

"Okay, better question," Keyon said, with a smile. "Where should we go to split it up?"

"Split it up?" Gerald asked.

"Yeah, split it up," Keyon said, with a grin. "I mean, you know that you wouldn't have found it if it hadn't of been for me and Jayson coming to Face Down."

"Yeah, you might have never come down here and found this, if I didn't get a job," Jayson said, with a nod.

Gerald looked at the bundle in his hands and frowned.

"Come on, Gee, you know that we split everything," Jayson said. He smiled broadly. "Everything."

Gerald took a deep breath and looked at the stack of bills in the plastic wrapping and shook his head.

"Great," Keyon said, with a big grin. "Where do you think we should go to count this shit out?"

"Well, we can't go to my house Gabi would lose her shit us showing up all late night," Gerald said.

"Yeah, we can't go to my house either," Jayson said.

"Okay," Keyon said, before Jayson could explain. "We know Wendy and Gabi ain't going to be happy to see us in the kitchen late night splitting this money." He paused. "Fine, then we go to my house, to split things up," Keyon said, annoyed.

"8 Mile it is," Jayson said, with a giggle.

"I don't live at 8 Mile," Keyon said as Gerald turned and headed toward Midtown. He knew driving through Midtown was the quickest way to cut through Detroit to get close to Keyon's Palmer Park condominium. The trip from downtown to Keyon's condo would take about twenty minutes.

Chapter 17.
Pancake

"**G**et out the car," Pancake said. He was a tall man. He was fit but not lean. Pancake was easily one of those guys who could work all day and play all night. In another time he might have been a gladiator or warrior. Naturally, he was intimidating. He had the dull look of someone akin to a human dinosaur. Pancake was a hammer. Not handsome or gifted with money or power he had been given every physical ability imaginable to survive.

Over six foot four inches tall and nearly three hundred pounds Pancake looked like one of the professional football players or TV wrestlers that were seen more on TV than in real life. There were few people as big and broad as Pancake.

Book and Mase could not help but look at Pancake like a modern-day superhero. Anywhere Pancake showed up, if there was violence or loud talk that violence and loud talk ended. No one wanted to test Pancake's physical prowess.

Pancake climbed out of the SUV and looked up and into the misting darkness, shielding his eyes with his big paw of a hand. Pancake opened the driver's side car door and turned off the engine. He turned and found Book and Mase on the sidewalk, waiting.

The big man pointed toward the store. In front of the store stood Delmar. He stepped into the driveway.

Mase and Book headed down the street and toward the store. The rain was increasing in its intensity again as the two boys reached Delmar.

"Nobody home," said Delmar.

Mase and Book lowered their eyes, silently.

"What you thinking?" Delmar asked.

Mase looked up and stared at Delmar, confused.

"It's okay," Delmar said as he stepped to Mase and placed a hand on his shoulder. "They should be close? Right?"

"Yeah, I think so," said Mase blinking, finding Delmar so close. He looked around the dark driveway and wondered what the cowboys were doing when they showed up? Mase shook that question from his head. He looked back toward Clark Street craning his neck and trying to get his bearings.

Delmar stood under the awning with a foot on a milk crate.

"They were hiding in here and jumped us over there," Mase said, remembering the attack.

"Okay," Delmar said. He looked to Pancake. Pancake looked around the quiet street as the rain fell. Delmar pointed across Clark Street toward the park. He began walking. Pancake followed.

"You two sit tight. We'll be right back," Delmar said.

The two gangsters crossed the street and looked down at the sidewalk. Delmar bent down and touched the ground. He climbed back to his feet and looked up and down the street for something. The pair looked through the chain link fencing surrounding the park and then back down to Clark Street. They talked and returned to the side of the street with the boys.

Book was standing in the driveway of the closed grocery store leaning against a wall when Delmar and Pancake returned. There was a flickering light going on and off sporadically overhead. Delmar beckoned the boys forward. Book hesitated. He moved beside the man who was three times his height.

"Okay, like I said, they can't be too far. Let's find these fuckwads who jumped you and see if any of them have our money," Delmar said and pushed Mase forward toward Clark Street.

Mase moved forward with the rough push and only briefly turned to glower at Delmar.

"You giving attitude little nigguh? To me?" Delmar smiled evilly. "You don't want to be on the wrong side of me, little nigguh."

Mase turned back and walked into the rain and onto Clark Street. He stood on the sidewalk not sure which way to go.

"Let's go south," Delmar said behind Mase.

Mase hesitated.

"Go right, little nigguh," Delmar said with frustration. "Damn, thought you were the smart one. Guess I got that wrong."

Mase gritted his teeth and turned right and walked down Clark Street toward Fisher Service Drive. There were no other buildings at the end of the block between the food store and the corner. Mase walked slowly to the corner, thinking that Delmar was going to kill him. He was walking, Mase thought absently, to his death. If he didn't find the cowboys that jumped him and Book, they both were dead.

"Stop at the corner, little nigguh," Delmar said behind Mase.

Mase refused to turn around and find Delmar with his pistol out and ready to blow Mase's head off. He walked and as he approached the corner thought to run left or right and try to outrun the bullet coming for him. Yet, at the same time, Mase thought that killing him meant that Book was dead as well. Neither he nor Book had fucked up before, Mase thought steps away from the corner of Fisher Service Drive. If they didn't find the missing bundle, then Mase or Book might be worm food. All they had to do was find one of the jackers and that would buy them enough time to not be buried in a shallow grave. At least, that was what Mase thought as he stopped at the corner of West Fisher Service Drive and Clark Street.

"See anyone that looks like the cowboys that jumped you down here?" Delmar asked.

Mase wanted to laugh. They were at the corner. There was no one out at the moment. It, the corner, was deserted.

Mase knew that Delmar was toying with him. He wanted Mase to turn around so he could shoot him in the face. So, Mase refused to turn around. He knew that Delmar had his pistol out and aimed at his head. He was just waiting for him to turn around to shoot him in the face. In his mind, Mase believed, that the longer he didn't turn to face his death the longer he would live.

"Nope," Mase said.

The rain was falling steadily now. Mase continued breathing and looking out into the night the rain falling but not as intensely as before. He looked across the street to the lighted underpass. If Mase ran across the street and he didn't get his head blown off he could hide in the underpass, but that possibility did not seem real. Delmar was close.

Delmar rested a hand on Mase's shoulder. He pushed his face over Mase's shoulder and looked at him with those dead eyes.

"So, tell me what you two were doing before these wannabe cow dicks jacked you?" Delmar asked.

"Nothing," Mase said. "We were just on the other side of Clark Street and figured it would be smooth sailing back to Choco—"

Delmar raised a hand and stopped Mase. He pointed to several dark figures walking through the underpass on the other side of the street.

"Is that them?" Delmar asked.

Mase looked into the darkness and tried to make out the figures but at the distance and dark and rain it made it nearly impossible to be certain.

"I'm not sure," Mase said, finally.

Chapter 18.
Nearly midnight

Keyon had come back to Detroit from Afghanistan with the hope of reconnecting with his friends. It, the idea of returning to his friends, had driven him while in the deepest and most chaotic situtations.

When he returned and reacquainted himself with civilian life Keyon had tried to consider where he should live. He couldn't live in his parent's house. That just wasn't a possibility. So, he stayed in a few low-rent apartments until he found his footing.

In Palmer Park there were some of the most amazing homes. There were some historic homes which sat on Palmer Park. Palmer Park was this little gem hidden in a small, insulated community with a forest, park, bike and walking paths and a little lake. The neighborhood had carved out its own distinct character and was close to the State Fairgrounds at 8 Mile Road.

Keyon lived in one of the much sought-after Albert Kahn condominiums, close to Palmer Park, in the shadows of Merrill Humane Fountain. His condominium rested a few blocks of Meijer and a string of recently converted condominium complexes which sat several blocks from the historic homes and apartments in the more elite areas of the neighborhood. The neighborhood was historic and under a developing resurgence.

He had been there for nearly two years and had no desire to move. His condo had everything a single man needed. There was a balcony which looked out toward treetops and the cityscape. He liked the seclusion.

His neighbors, the ones he met coming and going, were young professionals. They worked crazy hours, like him. Unlike Keyon they worked banker's hours, generally. They partied on the weekends but during the week it was usually library quiet.

So, while Keyon was working the majority of the condominium were sleeping. When he got off and was going to bed, they were hours away from waking and starting their days. His work schedule did not coincide with any in the condominium. He had only met the handful of people he knew by face on his days off. Keyon did not mind. He kept to his self.

On the fourth floor of his love shack Keyon Lewis resided with no strings attached.

"Welcome to my fortress of solitude," Keyon said as his two closest friends entered his home.

Key's condo was a big place for one guy, Gerald thought but never said because everyone else did. The condo sat in throwing distance of the Merrill Humane Fountain, but on the more affordable side of Palmer Woods. The condo had thirteen rooms including three bedrooms and three bathrooms. One of the rooms was a Florida room. The kitchen was a nice size, but it was the dining room which led to the gigantic living room which made the condominium incredible. The living room was arched and had built-in shelving, bay windows and a fireplace and felt like it was half of the spacious two thousand six hundred and thirty-nine square foot home of Keyon Gray. It was one of the reasons he had bought it along with the surprisingly tranquil view of the Palmer Woods where occasionally beams of lights might be seen.

"You say that every time we come over," Jayson said carrying his paper bucket of quarters with him.

"Why did you bring those quarters in here?" Keyon asked with a shake of his head.

Gerald chuckled and looked back to see Jayson with his bucket of quarters. He snickered at the sight. He made his way to the dining room and found the dining room table. He sat and took out the plastic bundle. The others sat down at the table.

Keyon had a counterfeit marker he had retrieved from somewhere.

"Okay, I'm going to say this once," Gerald said, looking at Jayson and Keyon. "I am only doing this because you were with me. I don't owe any of you shit. So, don't think that this is Gabi or that you are punking me into splitting this with you."

Jayson looked amused. Keyon chuckled.

"I am good to just say fuck it and walk out and not give two fucks if you both feel butt hurt over the whole situation," Gerald said. He was deadly serious.

"Fuck that," said Jayson.

"I found the money. I don't have to split shit with anyone."

"That's how you feel?" Keyon said, looking at Gerald oddly.

"That's how I fucking feel," Gerald said, his voice strained. He added, "I don't have to split shit with you Keyon."

"Fuck you Gee," Keyon said, his cackles up.

Gerald stood up. Keyon stood up as well. Jayson, the last to climb to his feet stepped between the two friends.

"Hey, both of you calm the fuck down," Jayson said, trying to be the peacemaker. "We boys. We been knowing each other forever. We splitting this to help each other out, plain and simple. It would be weird any other way. You both know that." Jayson took a beat looking at Gerald and Keyon. "You both calm the fuck down. We all would have split this shit if it would have been anyone else to find it, Gee."

Keyon stared daggers at Gerald.

"Sit down. Calm down. We all cool. We all good," Jayson said.

Keyon was the first to sit back down.

"Come on, we all come up together," Jayson said, appealing to his friends. "That's our thing."

"I'm serious," Gerald said, looking at his lifelong friends.

"Yeah," Jayson said, looking at Keyon. Keyon reluctantly agreed.

"We go way back and splitting this ain't going to make or break me," Gerald said. "It ain't like I'm rolling in it, but I ain't a nigguh that is going to squeeze on my money so tight that I can't share."

Jayson smirked and looked at Keyon. Keyon smirked.

"Are we going to split this shit or are you going to talk us to death?"

Jayson took a breath and laughed. Keyon watched Gerald.

"Well, the way I see it we got to establish some ground rules. We count this all together. Ain't no disappearing and then saying you didn't get a fair cut. Once we split this don't nobody come asking me for shit," Gerald said with a scowl. He was looking at Jayson.

"Why you looking at me?"

"How much you owe me and Gee right now?" Keyon asked.

"When we split this shit you and Gee are the first to get paid," Jayson said.

Gerald had a knife Keyon had brought from his kitchen. The knife was on the table. He picked up the knife and inches from the bundle he paused. A small worry line creased his forehead. He sat the knife on the table where the three had gathered.

"We doing this?"

"Hell, fucking, yeah, we doing this," Keyon said.

Jayson grinned.

Gerald lifted the knife and paused again.

"You know this ain't *our* money," Gerald said.

"Fuck that," Keyon said. "It's found money. It's found and now it's *our* money."

"Yeah," Jayson said.

Gerald agreed. He looked at his two friends. He studied them for a long moment.

"Like you said it's *found* money. Someone may come looking for it," Keyon said.

"If they come looking for it, they ain't going to find it. My shit is going directly into a bank."

"A bank?" Keyon asked.

"You can't deposit all this money at one time in a bank," Gerald said, his voice ratcheting up a little louder than he planned.

Jayson looked at Gerald with a smirk.

"All sorts of red flags will come up on a deposit over ten bands," Keyon said. "I should know. I'm in the cash business right about now."

Jayson waved Keyon off. He looked at Gerald and Keyon and tried to concentrate. "I been thinking about this since we climbed in the car," he said finally.

"A big deposit will be taxed too," Gerald said. Thinking of the problem with a lot of cash on hand.

"I know all that," Jayson said. "I ain't new. Give me some credit." He looked at Keyon and said, "I'm going to get a safe deposit box in the morning and put the cash in that deposit box. Then when I want it, I can dip in and get it."

Keyon grinned. Gerald slowly bobbed his head as well.

"Okay, are we good?"

The pair across from each other agreed.

"Okay, let's split this shit up."

Keyon checked the first five thousand dollars and finding them all genuine stopped checking. Gerald was in charge of splitting the money. Jayson checked the next thousand and found that they were dealing with real money.

From the initial count there was one hundred thousand dollars sitting on the table in front of Jayson, Keyon, and Gerald. Gerald split the bundle of bills into three even stacks of cash.

"Okay, that breaks down to thirty-three thousand a piece," Gerald said.

Each friend suddenly had three hundred and thirty bills in front of them. Gerald had three hundred and forty bills in front of him.

"No," Keyon said. "That's only ninety-nine thousand," he corrected.

"Right, I get the extra thousand for finding the stack," Gerald said, annoyed with Keyon.

"What about me? Don't I get to get a little more for splitting location?"

"Fuck no," Gerald said.

Keyon looked at Jayson.

"We could have counted it in a garage," Jayson said.

"Fuck you both," Keyon said. "Don't forget to give me that gee you owe me," Keyon said to Jayson.

Jayson looked smug and peeled off ten one-hundred-dollar bills and handed them to Keyon.

"You happy?"

"You got your extra band," Gerald said with a smile.

Keyon smiled disparagingly.

"Okay, shit is divided," Gerald announced. "Jayson, you got some plastic bags we can use to put our stash in?"

"Of course, he does," Jayson said with a laugh. "He work for the dope man."

Keyon climbed to his feet and walked into the kitchen and brought back half a dozen quart sized plastic bags.

"Perfect," Gerald said. He slipped his stack of bills into the plastic and sealed it. Jayson did the same thing with his stack of bills. The only one who didn't was Keyon.

"Okay, when we leave tonight, we didn't find shit," Keyon said, as Gerald and Jayson climbed to their feet.

"That's fair," Jayson said, with a smile.

"Fuck yeah, that's fair," Gerald said, adjusting his glasses.

"We can't have this money coming back on us," Keyon explained.

"Remember, don't let no one know," Gerald said. "Even your girl." He paused, thinking. "They would be the first one to start telling their girls how you and she came up on some money on the street."

"Shit would unravel," Jayson said.

"Real quick," Keyon said. "Sometimes there is a benefit to being just the one and only Keyon."

The two others looked at Keyon and shook their heads.

"So, this is going to be a nice little cushion for the remainder of the year," Jayson said. "It gives me a chance to breath and think about moving somewhere nicer."

Keyon agreed.

"What about you Gee?" Jayson asked.

"What about me, what?" Gerald asked.

"What you going to do with your cash?" Jayson asked.

"Yeah, I think that whole safety deposit box plan is starting to sound good," Gerald said.

"What you going to do with your cash?" Jayson asked Keyon.

"Might sit on it. Put it in my safe and wait shit out," Keyon said. "I ain't got no bee—woman to worry about going through my shit, like the two of you." Keyon paused. "I got the luxury of bachelorhood."

"Whatever nigguh," Gerald said. "I ain't got no ring on this finger," he said lifting his left hand.

"No but Gabi got a ring through your nose," Keyon said with a big laugh.

Jayson laughed at Key's joke. Gerald only shook his head.

"How you laughing?" Gerald asked looking at Jayson quizzically. "Wendy got two rings through your nose if Gabi got one through mine."

Keyon laughed at Gerald's words.

Jayson reluctantly laughed as well.

All three laughed, breaking the tension.

"We all just need to stay below the radar," Gerald said.

"What you going to do with your cash?"

"I think I'm going to lock it up. I thought about locking it up in the M3, but I would feel like shit if tonight of all nights they broke in and stole my shit. So, I was thinking of locking it up in the apartment and then in the morning go to the bank and get that safe deposit box."

"Okay, we all got plans," Keyon said.

The three looked at each other suddenly exhausted.

"You want a drink?"

Jayson and Gerald looked at each other.

"Naw, it's late, should head home. Got to drop off Jay," Gerald said climbing to his feet. Jayson climbed to his feet and grabbed his plastic bag of bills. Gerald held his bag of bills in his hand and shook his head.

"That's a lot of cash," Jayson said.

"Fuck yeah it is," Gerald said.

"Is that how much you make in a year?" Keyon asked.

"No, but it ain't something to sneeze at either," Gerald said.

"Yeah, that's right," Keyon said.

Chapter 19.
Velma and Shaggy

The two figures were on the far side of the street. One of them was wearing a long coat. Mase noticed that the dark figure was wearing boots. But the boy in the long coat could have been anyone. Then Mase saw the white girl.

"That them?" Delmar asked, pointing to a skinny white girl in her plastic outfit and a dark boy wearing a trench coat.

Mase and Book, now by his side, moved their chins up and down.

"Not all of them," Mase said, trying to be correct.

Delmar looked delighted at the good news. He smiled evilly at the greenlight he received from the two runners with the recognition of the jackers.

"Stay here," Delmar said. He pushed past Mase and Book. He bounced across the service road at an angle and before the two had reached the stairs Delmar was climbing up to them.

Pancake rested a heavy hand on Book and Mase's shoulders and watched as Delmar crossed the street and stepped to the pair. There was a short exchange between Delmar and the two strangers. The dark boy with the big ears which stuck out from his V-shaped head was the first to react to Delmar.

He swung and Delmar dodged the punch and dropped him with a short punch to the face. Before the skinny white girl could react, Delmar had his pistol out and aimed at the white girl's face. She had managed to pull her knife out. Delmar gestured for the girl to drop the knife. She dropped the knife and Delmar punched her.

Delmar tipped his head to the girl and smiled contemptuously. At that gesture Pancake ushered the boys across the street to the scene Delmar was lording over.

"This them?" Delmar asked.

"Yeah," Mase said.

Pancake stepped forward and over the unconscious boy. Mase and Book stood on the underpass walkway blocked by Pancake's bulk.

"It itches," Book said. Book lifted his sweatshirt and checked Delmar's handiwork. The dressing was a brownish red from dried blood. Book touched the spot and winced.

"You'll be fine," Mase said. "Stop messing with it."

Mase looked down and took in the boy who looked like he was sleeping bleeding on the sidewalk with a nose ring and a stud earring. His trench coat was all twisted and his hobnail boots looked beaten-up and in need of repair. Mase noted it was the same boy he had fought earlier because he still had the spiked dog collar on his wrist.

"Okay, bitch, where's my money?" Delmar asked.

The skinny white girl laughed. She laughed like she was high. Mase looked at Book and then Pancake trying to think what they were going to do with a crazy white girl?

Delmar slapped the white girl. Mase didn't see it. He heard it.

The girl crumpled on the underpass walkway and once on the ground reached for something in her boot. Pancake twisted whatever she had out of her hand. Pancake simultaneously pulled her back onto her feet.

"Little bitch, you think you going to leak me?" Delmar asked, stepping forward angrily. The white girl recoiled. Delmar raised a hand suddenly irritated by the white girl. "I can beat the white off you and not feel bad about it." He paused, studying the girl in front of him.

The white girl still dressed as Mase and Book recalled before, seemed skinnier and bonier. Her eyes seemed bigger too. Maybe, Mase thought, she was high or just coming off a trip.

"Where's the cowboy?" Delmar asked.

The white girl having been relieved of her knife and a derringer hidden in her boot was sullen. A trickle of blood sat on her pointy chin from Delmar's slap. She had big drug fiend eyes and crooked teeth.

Pancake stepped on the boy on the ground Delmar had knocked unconscious and the boy did not move. For a moment Mase thought the boy was dead. Then his hand moved and Mase knew he was still alive, just dreaming.

Pancake held onto the skinny girl's wrists as Delmar tried to figure out what his next steps were. He watched her reaction as he tried to decide what to do.

"You were heading somewhere? Let's drag this piece of shit and you to the most logical location," Delmar said scanning the street suddenly for possible places the cowboy crew might hang out in the rain.

"You ain't smart enough to go too far," Delmar said, with a smile. "So, if you went a block that would be too far. Now, is your hideout this way?" Delmar asked looking up Clark Street.

The white girl did not react.

"Or is it that way?" He asked looking in the direction the two had just come from, through the underpass. Delmar studied the girl easily and watched her every movement. He was looking for a sign or indication of something. Delmar looked toward the left of the underpass.

The white girl's eyes widened just a little. Delmar smirked. His eyes were the first to signal the eventual and eerily Cheshire cat smile from the slick street operator at the girl's reaction.

"Okay, white girl, I got a direction. Now, you can make this easy or hard. All I want to do is talk to the cowboy." He paused. "You look like one of those fucked up bitches that wants me to smack you around a bit." Delmar shook his head, looking at the white girl. "You would probably enjoy it and get off from it." He paused and looked at the barrenness of the dark area the two had just emerged from. "So, your friends waiting on you and Junebug to return?"

The white girl stayed silent. Delmar smiled smugly at her attempted bravery.

"It don't really matter if you talk or not," Delmar said. "I figure that in the next few minutes it's up to you who lives or dies." He paused. "Ain't shit out here. In a few minutes we going to find your hangout and either I am annoyed when I show up or I'm calm. You get to make that decision Goldilocks."

The white girl didn't say a word.

"Should I get the car?" Pancake asked.

"Naw, it can't be that far," Delmar said.

He looked at the white girl.

"You got a name?" Delmar asked the girl.

"Velma," the skinny white girl said with a crooked snarl.

"Velma? Okay," Delmar said with a chuckle. He looked at the girl in front of him and smirked. He reached out and Velma recoiled at Delmar's hand. He nodded. Delmar smiled patiently and studied the girl and then the boy lying at his feet. "Velma and Scooby didn't travel too far from the others." Delmar slipped his gun back in his waistband and took control of the girl. He pushed her forward.

"Bring Shaggy, just in case they need convincing we're serious," Delmar said to Pancake.

Mase and Book watched as Delmar shook the girl to get her attention.

"I ain't the baddest guy you going to see tonight, right now. But Velma, I got to remind you that there's no screaming or stupidness trying to warn your crew," Delmar said. "I ain't afraid to leak you if you act foolish."

Velma nodded. Delmar smiled pathetically at the bony girl with the big eyes.

Delmar looked back at Mase and Book. "Keep up little nigguhs, tonight you in for a real lesson in the game."

Mase walked with Delmar, looking back he watched as Pancake bent down and grabbed the foot of the still unconscious bad boy in the trench coat. He followed Delmar and the nameless girl through the underpass and toward the lone house on West Fisher Service Drive.

Book and Mase look at each other and Mase fell in behind Delmar as he pushed the white girl up the street.

West Fisher Service Drive was just a frontage road with a bunch of buildings up and down its length, but just a few blocks from the underpass stood a solitary house with lights on in the two-story structure. It was the only house on the frontage road.

"What time is it?" Book asked.

No one answered.

Chapter 20.
Midnightish

It was a little before midnight when Jayson and Gerald returned to the M3. The air was crisp and the streets quiet. The block where Keyon lived was dark except for the four or five streetlights. As the pair reached the BMW, they both looked around them to be sure no one was around and climbed into the sleek car. Once inside Gerald started the car and Public Enemy's *Black Steel in the Hour of Chaos* rumbled to life in the interior of the M3.

As the pair drove away from Keyon's condominium, they listened to the street poetry of Chuck D delivered over the musical genius of Terminator X.

Gerald and Jayson drove from Palmer Park listening to the greatest music of the Twentieth Century.

The pair drove to the M-10 South and climbed on the smaller state road. The road was quiet at that time of day. There were cars out but none that caused traffic of any kind to slow.

From Keyon's condo to Jayson's curb was just thirteen minutes.

"What you thinking you going to do with your half of the money?" Jayson asked.

"Hell, Jay, I can't say for sure," Gerald said as he drove.

"I think I'm going to get me and Wendy out of that apartment," Jayson said from the passenger seat.

Gerald nodded as he drove.

"I mean, I got a new job. I should be thinking about the future," Jayson said, leaning back in the leather seat.

"I guess," Gerald said, unsure.

"What you thinking about?" Jayson asked.

"I just want to stay under the radar for a minute," Gerald said. "I mean, I get the whole idea of thinking about getting out of the apartment but be easy."

"Yeah, I know," Jayson said. "I just want to put the money to some good use before it disappears."

"I get it," Gerald said. "I do."

The BMW fell quiet for a block or two.

"I was thinking about investing my money," Gerald said. "You know in the stock market?"

"Don't know nothing about that," Jayson said, looking from the passenger window back to Gerald.

"Yeah, I only know a little and a little knowledge is dangerous," Gerald said as he drove looking for Canfield Avenue. "The best way to increase your money is in the market. In this nation that's where all the money is being made. It's fucking crazy if you think about it."

"How?" Jayson asked.

"I don't know that much about it, but I know the general idea is that the market is all about the companies that we buy from," Gerald said. "The shares are a part of the companies that we buy from." He paused, turning onto Canfield. "We could invest in the companies we already buy from regularly and make money."

"Thought that was for the rich," Jayson said, unsure.

"It is, but it is also how to become rich," Gerald said. "The rich give their kids stocks and bonds for their birthdays. They get them cake and shit, but they are thinking about the future." Gerald paused, thinking. "The rich invest in their futures. They set up trust funds and give their kids stocks and bonds. We buy our kids Jordans and cars and think we are doing something." Gerald shook his head at the idea. "I read how the rich set up these trust funds for their kids when they are born, and they drop a mill or two for their kid and let that money gain interest for eighteen or twenty-one years and when their son or daughter is old enough to prove they understand the power of money they say here's ten or twenty mill."

"Gee, we ain't got that," Jayson said.

"True, but we got to start somewhere," Gerald said. "So, I'm thinking about investing my cash. I might start with ten. I mean I can lose ten and not feel it. It ain't my money. It's found money."

Jayson listened as the M3 rolled easily through the early morning.

"Do you need to have a stockbroker to help you with the stocks?" Jayson asked.

"Used to," Gerald said as he approached Woodbridge. "Things have changed. You can read and watch some videos and talk with some of us trying to climb up out of this national created poverty." Gerald paused. "There's a bunch of people to talk to for free. You know? It's advice. So, you take what you want and throw away all the bullshit." Gerald paused as he turned onto Warren Avenue. "The coolest thing is that if we pick the right stocks, we start stacking cash. We can stay in long-term like the Richie Riches or Scrooge McDucks or get out after we make our money back." Gerald pressed the brakes of his car. "It's the real hustle, you ask me."

Jayson smiled big in the passenger seat.

"Thanks Gee," Jayson said as Gerald pulled up to the curb.

Gerald agreed.

"No, I mean it," Jayson said. "Thanks for tonight and everything else."

Gerald chuckled.

"You said it earlier. You didn't have to split this with us," Jayson said.

"We boys," Gerald said. "We look out for each other."

"Yeah," Jayson said and closed the car door and spun on his heel to step onto the sidewalk and climb up the three short steps to the walk which led to his entrance to his basement apartment.

Chapter 21.
A Few Minutes After Midnight

"Velma, I am going to give you and your crew a chance to walk away from all of this alive and breathing," Delmar said. They had only walked a few feet and Velma seemed a little anxious.

"How you going to do that?" Velma asked.

"Well, that's pretty got damn simple," Delmar said. "The way I see it you know what we're looking for and you know if your crew got it, but we need to see for ourselves. If you let us do a look see and we don't find shit, then we're in and out and gone. But if you decide to play all crazy stupid then we're still going to go in but when we do, we're going to wreck shit from door-to-door."

Velma didn't speak for a second.

"You know I ain't bullshitting. Right?" Delmar asked.

Velma slowed her pace as the group reached the edge of the solo home on the street. The odd group of Delmar, Mase, Pancake and Book stood just a hundred feet from the house with half a dozen cars parked nearby. Mase close enough to the cars noted that most of the cars had no wheels or doors. They were hulls of cars.

The house was one of those houses that hadn't been touched by the invisible tornado, Mase figured, but being close to it the cars had been hit taking their wheels and doors while people weren't looking. Mase noticed that most of the cars were really old. There was a Pinto and a Gremlin rotting on the front lawn. They were all he noticed that night.

Delmar stopped Velma and looked left and then right. The house sat off the street. Delmar pointed at the bus stop bench in front of the house. Across the street was a Subway sandwich shop.

"Is this your clubhouse, Velma?" Delmar asked.

Delmar looked at Velma. Behind them Pancake was still holding the unconscious thug who Mase had fought earlier.

"You got to make some decisions, Velma," Delmar said. He tapped the girl on her temple. "I ain't got a lot of time. So, make good decisions or suffer for the wrong decisions."

Velma turned and looked at Delmar.

"Okay, okay," Velma said, trembling. "Promise me that you are just going to do a look see and if you don't find anything you will leave us alone."

"Look at me, Velma," Delmar said with a malevolent grin. "I am a man of my word."

"Okay," Velma looked back and took in Pancake and the unconscious thug on the sidewalk and the two boys in hooded sweatshirts and jeans. She looked back at Delmar. "We're on the second floor. There's usually two or three of us in the living room."

"Guns?" Delmar asked.

"Think Cecil has a gun and maybe Lamar," Velma said.

"How many in there right now?" Delmar asked.

"Tex, Cecil, Lamar and Bobby," Velma said, nervously.

"Okay, remember if you are fucking with us, I have to become one of Satan's devils," Delmar said.

He pushed Velma up the dead grass lawn and to the stairs. Delmar and Velma climbed the stairs together to the front door. Delmar pulled his pistol from his waistband, ready for anything.

"Open sesame," Delmar said with a devilish smile.

Velma turned the doorknob and pushed the door open.

Delmar pushed the pencil thin white girl wearing a transparent plastic get up into the house. He walked in behind her with his gun at the ready.

* * *

Gerald sat in the M3 and watched as Jayson walked to his door. He listened to the end of the music waiting for the next song to begin. While he waited, he could not believe the night he had with Jayson and Keyon. It was definitely memorable.

He checked the dashboard and noted the time. It was late, much later than he had planned on being out, but there was no other way to deal with things after finding the bundle.

Gerald texted Gabriella and told her he was just leaving Jayson. He planned on being home in ten to fifteen minutes. He didn't wait for Gabriella's response. It didn't matter. He was going to be home pretty quickly. He just needed to go.

Yet, he hesitated. He looked at the darkened house where Jayson lived and thought what had happened. Everything was suddenly different thanks to the discovery of the bundle of cash.

Gerald wondered, idly, if anyone was going to looking for the money? Of course, whoever lost that bundle was going to be looking for that money. The question was silly, even Gerald knew that.

Luckily, Jayson and Keyon did not live in the area and did not go to Face Down without Gerald, as far as Gerald knew. So, there was no way to connect them to the found money. At least, that was what Gerald thought.

He wondered who would have lost a bundle of cash? Whoever lost it was not going to be happy. If they traced it back to Gerald things would not be good. People losing that kind of cash were not the people that negotiated. They would torture Gerald or Jayson or Keyon for their money.

Instantly, Gerald imagined the worse tortures. He could see one or all of them tied up somewhere, in an empty warehouse, beaten to a pulp and someone with a knife or an acetylene torch threatening to remove body parts until someone talked. The idea gave Gerald the shivers.

He looked up and through the windshield and noted the light sprinkling of rain. The rain made Gerald shake the torture thoughts from his mind for the instant. Gerald considered where he would go to get a safe deposit box. He also wondered when the bank opened.

As he sat in the M3 he wondered if every bank had a safety deposit box.

Eric B and Rakim coughed and growled and came on with the ghetto anthem *I Ain't No Joke* and Gerald pulled away from the curb. He drove down West Warren Avenue and considered turning around in the neighborhood.

The M3 slid down the street and at the first light Gerald moved into the left lane and turned. He thought about doing a U-turn but thought twice about it. He would be the one to do a U-turn and get caught by some policeman he didn't see posted just a block away. So, instead Gerald turned left and made three quick lefts to return to Warren Avenue to turn right and head back toward Wayne State and his abode.

When he drove away from Jayson and the quiet of Woodbridge it was Friday, the thirteenth and still not one o'clock. What a night, Gerald thought. He had come up with thirty-four grand, thirty-five when Jayson paid him. Keyon had thirty-four grand and Jayson, happy go lucky Jayson, had thirty-one grand. Some night.

He expected to be home in ten to fifteen minutes if he made all the lights back to Sherbrooke Apartments. He planned on being in his apartment and in bed no later than one o'clock. It was a fair plan.

"Of course, the best laid plans of mice and men go awry and leave us nothing but hurt and pain for their promises of joy," Gerald said as he drove home that Friday morning.

Chapter 22.
Witching hour

Pancake dragged the unconscious boy up the stairs unconcerned about if the boy was alive or dead. Pancake stepped across the threshold and deposited the bleeding boy inside the front door. He was bleeding from his head, Mase noticed as Pancake pushed by him. Book followed Pancake. Mase turned around and entered the strange home wordlessly.

Once inside the dimly lit interior Mase and Book could make out two guys sitting on a couch. Delmar had his gun aimed at the two unmoving boys and the third holding a game controller. Delmar was all smiles. He had his arm around the shoulder of the skinny white girl in her plastic get up.

On the ratty couch two of the cowboy jackers were frozen. They had been playing a video game on a large monitor it seemed when Delmar and Velma appeared. There was the third one in the room still wearing headphones and who was blinking in a ripped-up lounge chair.

Pancake stepped into the living room and examined the three circling the monitor.

"You got this?" Delmar asked, not looking at Pancake.

Pancake nodded and studied the three like a butcher. Book was near the monitor looking at the game system and the games.

Out of the rear of the house, came the cowboy, wearing a cowboy hat, carrying a plate of cold cuts and two beers. He stood frozen, like he had been caught playing freeze tag, when Velma and Delmar appeared.

"This the cowboy?" Delmar asked.

The boy in the cowboy hat swallowed, confused.

Delmar reached out and grabbed Velma by the scruff of the neck. He immediately aimed his gun at the lone cowboy in the hallway.

Mase watched the two sides of the suddenly tense house. He was behind Delmar and Velma. To his left was Pancake and Book and the three jackers.

Mase looked from the cowboy and back toward Pancake and Book to see the giant take two quick steps to cross the space to the couch. He punched one of the two seated on the couch hard in the jaw, putting him to sleep instantly. The other jacker instantly jumped to his feet and tried to escape. Pancake, the gladiator, grabbed the boy by the arm to redirect him from the couch and fling him into the boy with the headphones in the chair.

The violence was like lightning. It was intense, unexpected, unbelievable, and instantly over. Mase took a step back as Pancake pounced on the two startled and stunned boys. The boy who was in the chair fell to the floor and there for the first time Mase saw a gun clatter to the living room floor. The gun had been in or under the chair.

Pancake slammed the boy from the couch into the wall and punched the boy in the chair unconscious and the other hard enough to make him rethink a fist fight. Pancake had lost his bucket hat somewhere in the brief, but intense brouhaha. Pancake climbed back to his feet with a scowl that threatened more violence on anyone willing to test him.

During the fight Book had jumped back and then ran forward to kick the boy still on the couch in the chest. As Pancake fought Book followed behind. When the gun fell out of the chair Book scooped it up. With Pancake surveying the scene he found Book with a gun. Book handed Pancake the gun.

Pancake tied the two would be jackers up. The big bald muscle-bound sepia hued thug was on the floor, bleeding from his nose from the punch Pancake had delivered.

Pancake smiled a smile which was more challenge than welcome at the bald and muscular thug on the floor. He looked around the living room and pointed to the game system. Book brought the game system to Pancake. He snatched the power cord out of the game system.

Pancake gestured for the muscle-bound thug to climb to his feet.

"Turn around," Pancake said, his voice sounded like gravel being crunched.

The muscular thug who didn't want any more of Pancake sat watching everything with hate in his eyes. He complied and Pancake easily restrained him and sat him on the couch.

The two who were unconscious Pancake grabbed and put on the couch with their friend. The boy with the two-inch-tall Mohawk, wearing thick glasses and sporting a nose ring was tied up with the game controller.

Delmar gestured with his pistol to the man in the hallway wearing the cowboy hat.

"Come out here, bad boy," Delmar said, his arm around Velma's shoulder.

The tall, thin brown cowboy with acne moved slowly forward. He had shed his two-piece rain suit, Mase noted. He was wearing one of those fancy cowboy shirts with button snap pocket flaps. On his feet still were his curled black cowboy boots.

"Velma, here's the thing," Delmar smiled, though the smile seemed painted on. "This is a big ass house. I ain't going to look all over. So, where's our money?"

"I don't know," Velma answered. Velma could have been in her twenties or forty-five.

"Fair enough," Delmar said as Pancake finished tying everyone up.

Book stepped forward and touched Delmar on the hip. Delmar looked down at Book.

"There's one more," Book said.

Delmar agreed.

"Don't need no heroes tonight," Delmar said dragging Velma toward the cowboy.

The cowboy looked at Velma with malice.

"Come on, cowboy, don't be that way," Delmar said. "This is business. Nothing personal. All I want is our money. If you got someone hiding thinking they about to save the day I would tell you to call off that airstrike or everything is about to get real red."

Delmar tapped the cowboy's temple with his pistol. The cowboy closed his eyes with the cold hard reality of the pistol against his temple. He swallowed.

"Web, come out, it ain't worth it. They got guns too," the cowboy said.

Web, the last member of the jackers was the dark figure who had been holding an umbrella and wearing a rain slicker. He was minus the umbrella and rain slicker when he appeared from behind a column, wearing a T-shirt, jeans, and sneakers.

Pancake walked toward Web. Pepper bristled upon seeing the mountain of a man approach.

"Be easy Web," Delmar said.

Pepper complied.

"Listen...," Delmar trailed off looking at the cowboy.

"Tex," the cowboy said.

"Sure, you are. Listen, Tex, we ain't trying to move in," Delmar said, sitting Velma and the cowboy on two rickety stools near the entrance to the living room. "You had a run in with our runners tonight." He gestured to the boys.

Tex studied the man in front of him. He looked at the giant and the two boys and accepted the situation.

"All I want to know is where is our money?" Delmar said.

Mase and Book stood looking at the controlled chaos in the wake of Delmar and Pancake. There was no screaming. There was no struggle. There was just control. There had been violence, but now, the violence seemed to be over.

"What?" Tex asked, confused.

"Your cowboy crew tried to jack our runners tonight," Delmar said, holding his pistol on the cowboy sitting unmoving on the stool next to Velma.

"What?" Tex repeated.

"This your bitch?" Delmar asked irritated suddenly.

"What?" Tex asked again.

Delmar shot his gun, frustrated. Everyone jumped, including Pancake. The bullet went into the wall harmlessly. Delmar looked at the cowboy steadily.

Book reached out for Mase. Mase brushed Book's hand away.

The cowboy was trembling. Velma seemed whiter than she was a minute ago.

"You listening to me? I ain't got time for twenty questions and this ain't Pulp Fiction," Delmar said, annoyed, but under control. He was not manic or unhinged and that in and of itself was chilling. "So, you tried to hijack my runners?" Delmar asked the pimply faced boy. "That's a yes or no question."

Mase gave a smug look at Tex with Delmar's words. Mase and Book were suddenly Delmar's runners.

"Yes," the cowboy said, frightened.

"Where's our money?" Delmar asked.

"We didn't get nothing from them," the cowboy said.

"Bullshit," Delmar said. "You know what happens when I hear bullshit?"

The boy opened his mouth looking at the hand cannon aimed at his face now and swallowed. "They were walking through our spot, and we know d-boys always use nobodies to mule dope or money. So, we took a shot." He quickly added, "But we didn't get nothing from them."

Mase watched Book watching Pancake like he was Michael Jordan or something. Pancake smiled cruelly over the musclebound thug. No one with two cents of a brain would fight Pancake, Mase thought. He was not the person you wanted to knuckle up.

Mase looked at the frightened white girl and the cowboy sitting on the flimsy stools. Mase looked at Book and saw how big his eyes were after Delmar had fired his gun into the wall. Mase closed his eyes and opened them again seeing Delmar smiling like he was Tex's friend.

He knew that most people would think that Pancake because of his size was the most dangerous of the two. But the man with the gun, no matter how nice he sounded, was the real danger.

"You took a shot?" Delmar repeated. He smiled. "You didn't get nothing from them?" Delmar asked with a knowing smile. "I can appreciate that." Delmar turned serious. "Where's our money? One of you peeled off one of our bricks."

The cowboy looked confused. He tilted his head, trying to make sense of what he had just heard. He looked at Mase and then Book.

"Wait, you think we got something from your runners?" The pimply faced cowboy asked, looking at Delmar. "They put up a fight. My girl stabbed one of them and if we could of we would of taken their packs but they ran away." He paused. The cowboy looked at Delmar evenly. "They didn't tell you that?"

"So, you saying none of your crew came back heavy?" Delmar asked.

"Yeah, that's what I'm saying," the cowboy said looking at Delmar.

Delmar paused and studied the cowboy. He was thinking, Mase could tell. Delmar tilted his head and looked at the cowboy again, a little closer.

"Pancake, watch him," Delmar said. Delmar turned and gestured for Book and Mase. Delmar walked to the hallway, just a few feet away from the scene of the chaos.

Mase and Book stood in the hallway. Delmar looked at the two boys seriously. He looked again like he might throttle Mase or Book or both. Delmar took a deep breath, thinking.

"Tell me the story from the moment you got jumped," Delmar said through clenched teeth.

Mase and Book retold their story.

"Well, like I said, we got jumped. I was on the ground. I got back up and grabbed my backpack and Book was running and we ran away. Book got his backpack."

"I got my backpack after that white girl stabbed me," Book interrupted. "That's how I got my backpack."

Mase looked at Book. Delmar looked at Book. Book studied the top of his sneakers.

"Yeah, so, we were running and nearly got hit by a car. We dodged a car coming at us and hit the side of a car and ran away from there. Then we were on Fisher, and I checked Book and then we ran to Ferdinand and found you and... you know the rest."

Delmar listened. He did not speak for a moment. He looked up toward the ceiling and back at the boys.

"Where did you hit that car?" Delmar asked.

Mase shook his head. "I don't know exactly," Mase said.

"Near that corner," Book said, remembering the neon lights.

"Yeah, by that bar," Mase said.

"The one we drove by?" Delmar asked.

"Yep," Book said.

"You sure?" Delmar asked.

"Well, we ran, and they were chasing us, and we nearly got hit by the car and Book bounced off a car and I bounced off the same car. The bar was right there," Mase said, recalling the events. He paused. "I'm sure."

Delmar exhaled, frustrated.

Chapter 23.
Back on the street

In Keyon's bachelor condominium he turned on his TV and checked out what was on. He was not tired or immediately heading to bed. He was used to getting home at late hours. So, Keyon walked to his couch and got comfortable in the leather cushions and flipped through the channels. He leafed through the channels and finding nothing to watch.

He climbed to his feet and went to the kitchen to look in his refrigerator for something to eat. Opening the right-hand door of his refrigerator he was greeted by a variety of choices. There was baked chicken, grapes, eggs, energy drinks, milk, juice, and pasta at eye level. He looked toward the bottom rack of the refrigerator and turned away uninterested in any of his food choices.

Keyon closed the refrigerator and opened a few cabinets only to decide to grab a glass and pour himself a drink.

"Hair of the dog," Keyon said to himself with a slight pout.

He replaced the whiskey bottle and proceeded to head out of the kitchen.

Keyon walked back into his living room pausing as he came parallel with the table where he and his friends had split the found money. Keyon looked at the money and chuckled.

"Thirty-three grand ain't chump change," Keyon said.

He pushed away from the living room to the couch. As he sat down, the TV advertising something Keyon did not want.

He sipped his straight bourbon and tried to imagine what had made that night spectacular. Nothing on TV and knowing Jayson was with Wendy and Gerald was locked down now that he was on his way home, the ex-military man, now a cannabis worker enjoyed the night with his friends.

He loved giving Gerald the business. It was lighthearted fun and never intended to be mean spirited. Gerald was a bit of a bookworm. Made sense, Keyon knew, as a teacher. Keyon loved digging at Gerald for some reason.

It was just the opposite with Jayson, Keyon realized. Jayson was incredibly talented but fighting a fight to be relevant in Detroit. The city was changing and had been changing for nearly fifty years. Jayson had the whole deer lost in the headlights feel to him, Keyon thought as he sipped his bourbon and decided to call it a night.

For a moment, he thought of calling Marisol. Instantly, he shook that thought out of his head. He placed the glass on the side table and chuckled at the idea of making a booty call. He was above that. At least, he told himself he was above that idea.

Keyon worked on a simple premise with women. If he was attracted to a woman, then he talked to her. If she was attracted to him, he would see where it went. If she was too clingy, she had to go. If he got too clingy, he had to let her go. Simple. Calling Marisol was a no no.

Keyon decided to call it an early night. He climbed to his feet and went to double check that his front door was locked. It was. Keyon laughed at his seemingly hyper cautiousness.

He laughed at the concern. He had brought money to his condo before but that night, that morning, it seemed different.

"Found money," Keyon said with a laugh, walking back from the front door only to pause seeing the three stacks of bills on the table that Gerald had left.

Keyon shook his head and looked at the Ziploc bag box and the three or four plastic bags on the table. He sat and meticulously slipped the three short stacks of cash into one baggie and before zipping it shut placed a hand on his windfall.

"Fuck," Keyon said in a whisper. "Got damn," he said a little louder, climbing to his feet and wanting to celebrate the newfound cash. He shook the idea from his head, for the moment, he walked away from the living room and past the black wrought iron grill of his fireplace. He turned off the TV and headed to his bedroom.

"Damn," Keyon said. He stripped out of his clothes and into boxers and a T-shirt.

In his bedroom, Keyon grabbed his remote and turned on the TV out of habit. The big screen blinked on and Keyon, as he had done in the living room, found himself flipping through the channels aimlessly. He knew that being in another room did not magically make the choices on TV different.

Bored. Keyon turned off the monitor and instead turned on the Internet radio. He flipped to his favorite R&B station and dimmed the lights. Before one o'clock he was asleep in his home alone.

*   *   *

Delmar and Pancake walked back to the Mercedes with Book and Mase following. Delmar was thinking about what the cowboy had said. He was also thinking about ending Book and Mase.

Pancake walked along at his slow gait. He did not seem to rush anywhere. Book and Mase followed along and as they reached the Mercedes the rain finally ceased.

"One good thing has come out of this night," Delmar said, spinning around and looking at Book and Mase angrily.

Book and Mase instinctually recoiled thinking Delmar was going to attack them.

"Okay, before we go to the bar," Delmar began and took a beat. "Are there any more things that you forgot to tell me about that run in back on Clark?" He paused and studied the boys. "Did you buy three beans from a stranger? Did you find a gingerbread house and stop to eat? Did you see a white rabbit?"

Book and Mase shook their heads in response.

"Are you sure?" Delmar asked.

Mase lowered his head. Book did the same.

"Okay, let me say this here and now," Delmar said in his easygoing manner. "If this is another wild goose chase, I'm not going to be happy. Me, not being happy, is not something you want to experience."

"We told you everything," Mase said.

133

"Obviously, you didn't tell me everything," Delmar said with a hiss. "If you told me everything, I wouldn't have wasted my time with the white girl and cowboys."

Book twisted his lips on his brown face. He reached out to Mase. Mase brushed off Book's grip.

"I know," he said to Book. "But they jumped us," Mase said.

"Yeah," Delmar said, with a nod. "I guess I would have had to come down here and put them straight about that. They can't fuck with our runners. It ain't that kind of party."

Delmar got quiet.

Pancake stood at the front of the SUV.

"We driving?" Pancake asked, his voice a surprisingly low growl.

"Naw, let's walk," Delmar said with a slight grin. "It's stopped raining. It's just a block up. It's just about closing time. No need to drive a block."

With that Delmar began to walk toward the hole in the wall bar sitting on a deserted side of the block.

As they crossed the street to the block where the bar sat Mase looked around and tried to recall how they had nearly been hit by a car.

"Remember? We were here," Book said.

Mase nodded his head.

"We jumped out of the way of the car and hit a car before running to Market," Book said.

The boys stopped. Delmar stopped. Pancake was the last to come to a stop.

"Look around," Delmar said. "Wouldn't it be our luck to find the stack on the ground."

The four searched the ground and Book was the first to see two dollars' worth of quarters on the ground. He tapped Pancake and showed him. Pancake looked down and picked up about a two dollars' worth of quarters and handed them to Book.

"Del," Pancake said with a growl. "Little man found a bunch of quarters on the ground."

"Quarters?" Delmar asked, narrowing his view.

"Yeah," Book said, raising the quarters to Delmar.

Delmar studied the quarters and the street they were on. He looked up and down the street for a reason to find quarters on the street. He looked across the street and then back in the direction they had just walked.

Looking at the small building with neon in the window and an unlit neon sign above the door Delmar smirked.

"Okay," Delmar said to Pancake. "Let's go and see if we can connect some dots."

Chapter 24.
Almost two o'clock

The bartender, Randolph "Randy" Ogden, rang the brass bell over the bar at one o'clock that morning. It signaled the last hour the local bar would be serving alcoholic drinks. He looked up and shook his head seeing there were only four people other than him and his wife in the dimly lit bar which had been around since 1987. He was nearly sixty and still in good health. Randy Ogden had a potbelly and needed to lose a few pounds, but for fifty-nine he was in decent shape, relatively speaking.

He did push-ups and sit ups and walked daily to fight the flab. Every night he opened the bar Randy wanted to be ready to handle whatever came his way. He was nearly five foot ten inches tall and felt that he was more than capable of handling anything that happened in the bar.

In the five years he had owned the bar he had been robbed only once. The robbery had been a lot of noise and gun waving and the robber had taken three hundred dollars and scared his wife. If it had been just Randy, he might have fought the robber, the bartender liked to think, but he had to worry about his wife, Amanda, the barmaid.

After the robbery Randy had bought a little protection. Underneath the bar was a loaded Mossberg shotgun. Randy always found himself looking at the shotgun in the closing hours of the night. According to the police the most likely time to be robbed was between one and three in the morning.

Randy Ogden did not imagine anyone would rob the local watering hole frequented by dock workers and cops on occasion. If someone decided to test Randy now, they would be sadly mistaken. Randy prided himself on being a good shot.

The bar's history was one of the reasons he and Amanda had bought the small watering hole. Lloyd Harris had been the original owner of the Port O' Call. He owned it from 1987 until 1997 when he got sick and before the New Year was dead. His family sold the bar to Stephen Lawton and in 1998 Lawton took over the Port O' Call and renamed it Portside. Lawton saw himself as an investor and not a bar owner and after just two years sold the bar to Anthony "Tony" Lawrence.

Lawrence held onto the small little bar now named Face Down from 2000 until 2010 when he was killed in a hit and run just a few blocks from his home in Lafayette. The bar was put up for sale by the bank and in 2011, just months after Lawrence's death it was in the hands of Scott Baker. Baker, like Lawton, saw the bar as an investment. He held onto the newly managed Face Down for just five years before selling it to Randolph "Randy" Ogden and his wife Amanda.

Amanda and her husband had bought the Face Down just five years ago. It had been a great deal, initially. It was another stream of income. She and Randy were recently retired and looking for something to spice up their lives.

The couple had considered renaming the bar, but everyone knew it as Face Down. It was an unofficial Port of Downtown landmark and watering hole and the couple had been the owners for just five years. The business was steady, and Randy could not complain about the surprisingly strong business at Face Down. It didn't hurt that the bar was the only bar in any direction from the waterfront to Vernor Highway and back to downtown.

Amanda Ogden cut her eyes toward the four regulars at the bar and beamed. They had been coming to the bar on and off since the couple took over the bar. They appeared, drank, never caused any trouble, and left usually leaving a decent tip.

Everyone who came to the local dive bar always talked about the first time they had come to the watering hole. The Face Down had been through several hands but the dockworkers loved the small bar. The original residents of Southwest Detroit who still remained loved the bar as well.

The barmaid eyed her husband and looked to the clock. It was nearly two o'clock. She raised her chin to him and walked to the rear of the bar and unplugged the slot machines. There were two tables in the rear of the small bar, and she grabbed the chairs and flipped them up and onto the table, closing down the back half of the bar. There were five small round tables in all, which meant there were three tables to clean up to shut down the bar. Of course, before leaving they usually mopped the floor. In a bar there was always a need to mop the floor.

Thankfully, Amanda thought, she was only responsible for the main bar and the women's bathroom. The bartender had to mop and clean the men's room before calling it a night. The barmaid thought all this as she looked over the four regulars.

"All right, gents," Randy said with a smile on his pudgy face. "We'll be closing up soon. Last round?"

Marvin Proctor, he lived alone and came by the bar two or three times a week. He was a quiet man. He was never a problem. He usually arrived late at night, after midnight, and stayed until just before close.

Marvin climbed to his feet and tipped his hat to Randy as he left. He lived in one of the old bigger houses on the other side of Clark Court, just behind the middle school. His family had lived in Southwest Detroit, he told her, since before they built the park. Amanda didn't mind Marvin's arrival or his attempt at being funny. He just seemed to be a lonely man who needed a little social interaction.

Sitting just a stool away from Marvin that night was John... Amanda knew the big man had told her his full name many of times but for the life of her she could not recall it. John... Redding, Amanda laughed to herself recalling the man's name. John Redding worked at the Detroit Parks and Rec.

Redding was a grounds maintenance man for the city. He was tasked with locking down the dozen parks in Southwest Detroit after ten o'clock each night. He always told Amanda how dangerous the grounds maintenance workers were. There was rarely a day went by that someone wasn't hurt because of misuse of their equipment, Redding told anyone who would listen.

The Southwest Detroit Parks and Rec center sat just a mile away from the bar and after his shift John Redding would appear. He usually appeared every night a little after midnight and at the end of his shift. He didn't drink hard alcohol. Instead, John ordered a couple of draft beers when he had a memorable night. That morning, after last call he climbed to his feet and left with a wave of his hand, heading home.

Billy Jenson was a security guard who worked somewhere on West Grand Boulevard and lived in Southwest Detroit. He liked to sit at the bar most nights and was always dressed in his security guard uniform with bulletproof vest. Billy was nearly fifty and graying. He had been married and divorced and now happily single. Billy always had two bourbon shots and left before closing. That night, he was the third soul to leave the Face Down.

The last to be in the bar that night was Jesse Howell. Jesse Howell was recently retired and in his sixties. He had been married and was now a widower. According to Jesse his wife, Marjorie, was an angel. They had met in high school. He had gone to serve. When he returned home, he had asked her to marry him. They had three children. All of them were grown and scattered across the state. Now, Jesse was all on his own. He was thinking of traveling to South America, something he had always dreamed of doing. Jesse would order a beer and sip it for an hour.

With Randy's announcement Jesse climbed off the bar stool he was occupying and headed to the door. He was wearing a raincoat, hat and carrying an umbrella.

The late-night shift crowd was a group Amanda imagined the bar would be attractive to, but they probably needed something glitzier and more glamorous usually found downtown in the trendier bars. Face Down was an acquired taste.

*　　*　　*

139

The Face Down was only 1,200 square feet from front to rear. Entering the bar there was a small foyer where coat hooks hung for coats. Making a sharp right most customers walked into the Face Down and were greeted by the end of the bar which stretched two hundred feet from the front of the bar to the round tables. Above the bar was a sectioned mirror gilded with filigree.

There was no one in the small bar when Delmar and Pancake stepped inside with Mase and Book trailing.

"Hey, guys, welcome to the Face Down, but sorry we're closing," Amanda said looking up and seeing the dark man smiling at her.

"Aw, can't you just be a deer and serve us one drink before you close up for the night?" Delmar asked, smiling sincerely. "It's not two o'clock exactly."

Amanda looked at the man and the three behind him and then at Randy.

Randy was wiping down the bar. He shrugged his shoulders.

"What'll it be?"

"Well, I'd like a rum and coke. What about you Pan?"

"I'll take whatever you have on tap," Pancake said sitting at the bar. Pancake sat on a barstool close to the door. Book and Mase hovered near Pancake.

Mase watched as the bartender looked at him as if he was trying to figure out how the four were connected. Mase took a few steps forward and leaned back against one of the barstools. Book rested his forearms on the barstool seat and then his head.

Delmar walked to Amanda, who was putting the chairs up on the tables, preparing to go. She studied the extremely friendly man dressed in a motorcycle jacket, collared shirt, jeans, and pointy shoes, who had entered with two children and a giant of a man.

Amanda looked at Delmar evenly. She looked at the giant of a man, now sitting at the bar, and the two kids and did not know what to expect. She studied the stranger in front of her. A line of concern appeared between her eyebrows.

"You getting anything for the boys?" The barmaid asked.

"Sure, sure," Delmar said, looking back. "Tell the bartender what you want," Delmar said to Mase and Book.

"Could I have a Coke?" Book asked.

Mase looked at Book and then back toward Delmar.

"What about you?" Delmar asked.

"Order something," Delmar said, impatiently.

"Can I have a Seven-Up?" Mase asked.

"Okay, that's it," Delmar smirked having waltzed to the middle of the small bar. Amanda stood and watched Delmar. Randy, the bartender, watched the two men carefully as he gave the giant his beer first. He eyed the Mossberg under the bar and measured the distance. It was within arm's reach.

Pancake sipped his beer and sat at the bar silent as death. Book continued leaning on the barstool. Mase touched the bar and felt the warmth of the wood.

"Is this all made of one piece of wood?" Mase asked.

The bartender did not answer. Instead, he continued wiping down the bar and watching the giant closest to him.

Book blinked and tried to stifle a yawn. Mase looked at Book and tried to stifle his own yawn. His yawn was contagious. Mase tried to shake the yawn off that Book had sent his way, but it was too late. Mase yawned too.

In the Face Down there was an old-fashioned Wurlitzer 2700 jukebox. It had about two hundred songs inside. Yet, it was on the far side of the bar, past the halfway point.

"Can I check out the jukebox?" Delmar asked with a friendly smile.

"Sorry," Amanda said, with a slight scowl. "As I said, we're closing."

"I understand," Delmar said with a smile. "It's going to take a minute to get my drink made and I just love old jukeboxes. It's sort of a thing for me." He said so innocently. "I just want to see the selection. I won't play it. Just looking." He added, with a sweet smile, "As soon as my drink is made, I'll drink and we're out as quickly as we showed up. Promise."

Amanda acquiesced and Delmar bowed to her formally and walked back to the jukebox. As he did, he noticed to the right of the jukebox there were three Las Vegas slot machines in the rear of the Face Down. The bar suddenly became interesting.

"You know that these are antiques?" Delmar said.

"You don't say," Amanda said.

"Yeah, the last time I looked I think they were selling for a cool two gees," Delmar said, looking at the selections on the jukebox. "My question is where do you get the 45s to play the songs?"

"Well, we don't change the selections too often," Amanda said, lifting a chair and flipping it to sit on top of the round table. Delmar was suddenly at her side. He reached out and helped the barmaid place the chair on the table.

Amanda was startled by the stranger appearing near her.

"I didn't mean to frighten you," Delmar said, smiling broadly.

"You didn't," the barmaid began.

"You got slot machines?" Delmar asked, interrupting the barmaid's response.

She looked into the dark corner of the bar and back to the stranger.

"They don't work," Amanda said, trying not to show the stranger she was lying. "They're just for show."

Delmar smiled sweetly. He looked at the barmaid and tilted his head, looking at her intently. Delmar nodded, smiling malevolently. He looked at the bartender and then Pancake and then back to the barmaid.

"I like a show," Delmar grinned evilly.

Chapter 25.
Del on steroids

Everything had gone from friendly to terrifying in seconds with Delmar signaling Pancake. The giant reached out to the bartender who was eyeing his Mossberg under the bar. Before Randy could move Pancake had the bartender halfway over the bar and knocking Mase and Book from beside their barstools in the effort. Pancake deftly smacked the surprised bartender once and the potbellied bartender went quiet on top of the polished wood bar.

"Lock the doors," Delmar said, looking at the boys. He turned and Amanda saw the business end of a 9MM pointed in between her liquid blue eyes.

Book and Mase scrambled to their feet. Each looked at the other. Pancake was suddenly sitting on the bar next to the still man dressed in a T-shirt which seemed too small. It showed off his pale skin below his navel to his waistband.

"I said, 'Lock the doors,' now lock it," Delmar said to the boys.

Book turned and of the two was first to run to the door and turned the bolt lock on the front door. He returned and saw the controlled chaos in front of him. Little had changed.

Mase was near one of the two round tables which still had chairs under them. Pancake leaned over the bar and came back with the nozzle of the refreshment bar. The giant studied the choices on the nozzle.

"Did you lock the door?" Delmar asked.

Book nodded his head.

"Good," Delmar said with a satisfied smile.

The white woman eyes looked as big as saucers as Delmar turned his attention to her. Delmar was the only one with a gun.

"Okay, sweetheart, I don't have a lot of patience with your kind," Delmar said, honestly. "I never have. So, I'm not going to take too much of your bullshit." He paused and studied the woman he had his gun aimed at. "What's your name?"

"Amanda," the woman dressed in a black T-shirt and jeans said, blinking her blue eyes at Delmar.

"Okay, Amanda, I have a couple of questions. I just want you to answer me honestly. If you can do that we'll be out of your hair, and you can go back to your life without me in it." Delmar smiled broadly. "You understand?"

Amanda, the barmaid, nodded her head.

"Okay," Delmar said with a friendly smile. "Did you have any big winners on the slots tonight?"

Amanda didn't speak immediately. Delmar studied her as she tried to think what to say.

"You are probably trying to think if you tell me the truth are they going to kill me or rape me or whatever?" Delmar proposed. He smiled without emotion. "Let me say that I didn't come here to knock off this two-bit bar I would never have been caught dead in. My plan has nothing to do with killing or raping anyone here," Delmar said. He paused. "Now, you have to decide if I am lying to you? I have to do the same with you. The difference is that of the two of us my opinion matters more."

Delmar paused and gestured for Amanda to sit down at the table they were near. The two sat at the small round table. Delmar rested his elbow on the tabletop to steady his arm and keep the gun trained on Amanda's face.

"Think Amanda," Delmar said. "The next thing you say could mean someone's life or death."

"We had a few winners tonight," Amanda said, tremulously. She was studying the 9MM just an inch from her nose.

"Now, you look like the brains of this business," Delmar said with a nod. "Pan, wake that fat fuck up. I need him awake."

Pancake pressed the refreshment nozzle and water splashed on the bartender. Seconds later he came to, disoriented.

Pancake put a big paw on his shoulder and slowly allowed him to sit up. Pancake deposited the blinking Randy Ogden on one of the barstools in front of the bar. The giant rested a hand on the bartender's head. He twisted the bartender's head toward Delmar and Amanda.

"Okay, now that we have both of your attention, I'm going to ask you a simple question. Pan is going to respond every time I don't like the answer."

Randy and Amanda looked at each other with pleading eyes.

"Do you pay out in quarters?" Delmar asked.

Amanda looked at Randy. Randy blinked.

Delmar seeing Amanda looking at the bartender for an answer instantly angered. He gestured to Pancake. Pancake squeezed the bartender's head.

The bartender moaned at the pressure applied to his head.

"How many people won big in the last two or three hours on those slots?" Delmar asked.

The bartender looked at Pancake and reached out as if he thought he could take on the street hardened giant. For his trouble, the bartender received one shot, not the hardest shot in Pancake's repertoire of punches, in the soft midsection of his unguarded potbelly. Instantly, the bartender was on his knees trying to catch his breath.

"Every time I have to ask the same question, I think I will have to break something," Delmar said. "Well, Pancake will break something." He smiled. "Let's start with a finger. I like the sound of those bones breaking."

Amanda's eyes widened at Delmar's calm. Amanda looked toward the bartender again.

"You keep looking over there and you're going to make me angry," Delmar said. He paused and studied the woman in front of him.

"I think you think I'm not serious. Okay. Okay. That's fair. Have to prove I am willing to do what I say. No threats? That's fair. I like you Amanda," Delmar said with an evil smile.

Amanda seemed visibly shaken.

"Not like that. I don't dabble," Delmar said. "Break a pinkie," Delmar said looking at Amanda.

Pancake grabbed the bartender's hand and without much effort snapped his pinky finger.

The bartender yowled.

Delmar smiled sadistically at the sound of the bartender's pain. He looked at Amanda bemused. He was about to speak when the bartender continued to moan. He groaned with tears in his eyes.

"Shut him up," Delmar said.

Pancake reared back and punched the bartender in the face and silenced him.

"Now, you got an answer?" Delmar asked.

After Pancake woke up the bartender to break another finger Amanda named the people who had won in the last three hours. There were only three.

There was Marvin Proctor. He lived in one of the old houses. He had only won about twenty-five dollars from the slot machines. He had taken the money as a cash advance on his credit card.

There was Billy Jenson had won about forty dollars from the slot machines. Billy like Marvin had used his credit card and asked for a cash advance to be debited on his credit card.

The third winner of the night was this black kid who came in every once in a while, with his friends named Jayson McKinley, Amanda recalled.

"Tell me more about this Jayson McKinley," Delmar said.

"Jayson McKinley won nearly fifty dollars and chose to get a cash payout in quarters," Amanda said.

Delmar smiled evilly. He looked at the boys and then at Pancake. He seemed satisfied.

"You got an address on this Jayson McKinley?"

The bartender regained consciousness and was holding his hand like a newborn baby.

Amanda hesitated. Delmar shook his head.

Pancake punched the bartender and made him spit blood from his mouth.

"I have to go to the bar and look it up. I think we capture his address and credit card information in case there is any irregularities," Amanda said, trembling.

"Isn't this whole thing an irregularity?" Delmar asked and then shook the question off. "I don't care. I want the address. No funny business."

Amanda walked behind the bar. Delmar followed her. He watched as she went to the cash register and punched a few keys.

"Don't do anything stupid," Delmar said, as a reminder. "We just need the address and we're gone. No muss. No fuss."

Amanda opened the cash register and then punched a few more keys and suddenly the screen on the register changed subtly. Delmar studied the cash register and smirked.

"They are always trying to get all the information they can," Delmar said. "Even in a place like this."

Amanda looked left and right, and Delmar pressed his pistol to the back of her head.

"What you doing?"

"I'm—I'm looking for a pen to write down the address," Amanda said, instantly raising her hands.

"No funny business," Delmar said.

Amanda nodded her head.

The barmaid found a pen and a napkin and wrote down the address to Jayson McKinley. She slowly turned around and found the 9MM again in her face.

"Stand right there," Delmar said, scanning the cash register information and the address the barmaid had written. Satisfied, he pushed the woman out from behind the bar.

"Okay, Amanda, we're about to leave," Delmar said.

He looked at Mase and gestured the boy to the bar. Mase didn't move. Book next to him elbowed Mase to get his attention. Mase looked at Book. The younger boy tipped his chin toward Delmar.

"Get the shotgun from behind the bar," Delmar said.

Amanda started to cry.

Delmar looked at the barmaid in disgust. He looked as if he had stepped in someone's sick.

"What's wrong with you?" Delmar asked. "You're one ugly ass crier. Don't cry. We just making sure you or... your hero don't get all

Death Wish and think you can gun us down on the streets after we leave."

Mase walked past Delmar and the bartender. He stepped behind the bar and after a minute returned with a shotgun.

"Give it to Pan," Delmar said, instructing Mase.

Pancake took the shotgun and still watching the bleeding bartender on the floor unloaded the weapon. Pancake lifted the shotgun in his hand and sat it on the bar, empty.

"Hold onto the shells," Delmar said to Mase and Book.

The two boys walked to the bar and picked up the shotgun shells.

Chapter 26.
Threeish

Delmar, Pancake, and the runners were driving to the address Amanda had given them. Delmar was smiling from ear to ear, like a kid getting ready to cut his birthday cake. Mase did not know what to think. So, he just sat in the front passenger seat and rode along, numb.

He had witnessed Delmar and Pancake handle business. They were unstoppable. They seemed to have no fear of anything. The pair were wrecking balls. Delmar was this demented and evil individual who did not believe there was a limit to his madness. He threatened. He tortured. He continuously grinned or smiled at the devastation he committed.

Pancake was no better. Pancake was the hammer. Delmar the carpenter. In Delmar's hands Pancake was a smashing and destructive force most were not ready to deal with.

"Okay, this is going to be some next level shit, little nigguhs," Delmar said. "You about to earn your stripes for real tonight," he said.

The four climbed out of the Mercedes Benz. Pancake stood on the sidewalk with his bearlike hands clutching at the air. Book was looking at Delmar uncertain what was happening. Mase looked up and down the quiet street a few minutes before three o'clock in the morning. There were no cars on the street, Mase noted.

"You two go around back and find us a way in," Delmar said.

Mase looked at Delmar and thought he was kidding.

"I ain't playing," Delmar said. He looked at Mase sternly. "Get going."

Mase blinked and looked at Pancake who seemed so far away all of a sudden. Mase looked to Book. Book didn't speak. His lips trembled.

"Come on," Mase said, turning on his heels and heading up the three stone steps to the walkway. Book reluctantly followed.

Once on the walkway there was a set of steps which led to the porch of the main house. Mase looked down the walkway which led to a door beneath the main house and walked to the right past the steps to the porch and to a wooden gate. At the gate Mase tried to open it only to find it locked. The boy climbed over the gate with the use of the neighboring fence.

Mase landed on the other side of the fence and a few seconds later Book landed beside him.

"This is bad," Book said.

"You think?" Mase said.

"What we going to do?" Book asked.

"We don't have much choice," Mase said, walking as quietly as possible into the dark backyard of the unknown house. As he moved into the backyard he pushed and tried to open any window available.

After a few minutes Mase and Book reappeared.

"Found a way in," Mase said.

"Good," Delmar said, pushing the two boys back toward the quiet house.

*   *   *

Jayson fell asleep in the arms of Wendy. The pair cuddled and surprisingly the last memory Jayson had was of the night with Gerald and Keyon. He fell asleep thinking how lucky he was to have those two personalities in his life. He had happened to find them when he was just in grade school. Like all things in his life, he had put little effort in to hold onto.

He never liked to admit it, but he was a black slacker. He had dreams. He had hopes. Jayson was not always motivated to make his dreams reality or to see his hopes through to their end. All his plans had been more impulsive.

Where he lived, in Core City, happened on a fluke. Woodbridge was a small bedroom community between Core City and

150

Midtown and just a short walk to the Motor City Casino. It was an older community and Jayson could not recall clearly how he had landed the basement apartment in the house of Emma Langston. Emma Langston was eighty and smart as a whip. Her son, Billy, visited her regularly and it was Billy who collected the rent from Jayson.

The basement apartment had its own entrance and was a complete one-bedroom apartment. The nine hundred square feet was divided into a small rectangular living room which doubled as a work area for Jayson and yoga area for Wendy. Against the living room wall were four computer monitors connected to two computer towers and two microcomputers. On the other side of the living room was the small and functional kitchen. On the opposite side of the small apartment was the spacious bedroom, bathroom and on the opposite side of the kitchen the small dining room area, where Jayson's and Wendy's bicycles hung.

The bonus, if there was any bonus, to the intimate apartment was a backyard. The yard let out into a small area where, the weather permitting, he and Wendy could just relax and be away from everything hidden by eight-foot-high hedges. The backyard was secluded and fenced off to the public. Emma Langston confessed she was happy to have a lodger.

"Use the backyard all you want," Emma Langston said. "If I come out it will just be to the back porch. You know I am eighty. I am a little more fragile than I care to admit. My son has forbidden me from walking down the back stairs for fear that I might tumble and break something."

"Well, Missus Langston, if you need anything just ask," Jayson said.

Jayson liked his property owner. She walked around above them, and rarely did he or Wendy hear her soft tread.

He and Wendy had been living in the basement for a little over a year. He had moved there after losing a job, getting hired and then losing that job to downsizing. To make ends meet Jayson was working at Best Buy as part of the Geek Squad team.

Jayson was a computer wizard. He had always been interested in computers. When he was in high school, he created a series of stop action films with clay and three characters similar to Gumby and Pokey. The twist was instead of Gumby he created a Grumpy character who was always grumpy. He had an always contradictory pal who was friends with Grumpy. That character was named Milk. The last stop action character was a hapless loser named Bo. Everyone in high school loved Chilling, the name of the inconsistent film anytime it came out.

For the longest time in high school there was a belief Jayson was going to go to film school and become a famous black animator like LeSean Thomas or Bruce W. Smith. Then reality sunk in.

Unfortunately, his grades did not get him to film school. Instead, after high school he went to a junior college and then dropped out. He bounced around. For a year he went to Chicago and tried to break into the business. He returned broken. Jayson worked at Best Buy for a year then out of nowhere he worked in a couple of small studios and got discouraged. He worked and scrambled and worked hoping for a break.

He had eventually found himself. Jayson looked for a graphic design shop which focused on music. It was there, six months in, he decided to give his animation dreams one last shot. He had cleaned up his Chilling portfolio and recorded a sizzle reel.

Jayson thought all this before he drifted off to sleep.

Hours later he woke hearing something which jarred him. The first sound was heavy. The following sound was light and bright.

"Wake up, Jayson," Delmar said poking Jayson in the side of his head.

Jayson blinked awake and seeing Delmar holding a pistol in his hand. Jayson sat up instantly alert.

Before Jayson could react, Pancake grabbed him and pulled him out of bed, like a rag doll. He was punched a few times in the chest and stomach by the smiling stranger. Jayson looked at him angry from the attack and was rewarded with three punches in the face.

A sock was stuffed in his mouth to stop him from yelling. His hands were jerked behind his back and his wrists tied quickly with a leather belt. Jayson could taste blood in his mouth along with the cotton of the sock.

Jayson was seated on the edge of the bed with a sock in his mouth and his hands bound. In his bedroom were four people, two men and two boys with Wendy.

Wendy was sitting in a chair dressed in her negligee with a sock in her mouth and her hands and legs tied by electrical cords recently ripped out of something.

The two boys stood near Wendy, unmoving. One of the boys was looking at Wendy barely clothed in her negligee. The other was holding the battered paper bucket from Face Down.

"You one sound ass sleeper," Delmar said with a smile. "That's a bad habit to have." He paused and looked at Jayson with a friendly look on his face. "Where's my money?" Delmar asked. "I found this but this ain't all of it." Delmar lifted the plastic bag filled with thirty thousand dollars. "We are light seventy large."

Book looked at Mase and leaned over to him. Mase pushed Book back and away from him with a shake of his head.

"I know. I know," Mase whispered holding the paper bucket filled with quarters. "I know you found the money. He don't care. He's making a point."

Jayson shook his head.

"I ain't got time to be all nice and friendly, Jayson," Delmar said. "I know you stole my money. I just want it back. It ain't yours. You have to have known someone ain't going drop a stack and not come looking for it," Delmar said with an evil smile.

Jayson mumbled something.

Delmar reached out with his left hand to remove the sock gag and stopped himself. He smiled playfully. In his right hand he held his pistol.

"Okay, here are the rules. If I remove that sock and you scream, I'm going to have to kill your bitch," Delmar said with a serious look. He looked back at the girl tied to the chair in her sheer negligee. "You heard me? If your nigguh can't hold his shit together then I'm painting the walls red with your brains. Sorry babe."

Delmar looked back at Jayson.

"We good?" Delmar asked.

Jayson nodded his head. Delmar removed the sock.

"Okay, where's the rest of my money?" Delmar asked.

Jayson blinked and tried to register all the people in his bedroom and the gravity of the situation he was suddenly in. The stranger with the gun placed the gun under Jayson's chin and lifted his head so they were eye level.

"Where's my money?" Delmar repeated with a smaller smile.

"Look, I ain't got your money," Jayson said, dressed in boxers.

"Do you want me to kill you?" Delmar asked, tilting his head.

Jayson did not respond.

"Do you want me to kill your bitch?" Delmar asked.

Jayson blinked, shocked by the question.

"I have had a long night dealing with a bunch of bullshit," Delmar said to no one in particular. "My patience is thin. So, I ain't going to be delicate about this. I ain't got time. Once I put that sock back in your mouth, I'm going to fuck you and your bitch up, plain and simple."

Jayson blinked.

Delmar grabbed the sock and jammed it back into Jayson's mouth.

"Okay, let's see how you like watching your bitch be... mistreated," Delmar said.

He climbed to his feet and walked to Wendy, sitting in the chair. Still holding his pistol Delmar placed the barrel of the gun against Wendy's temple. He looked back at Jayson unsympathetically.

Jayson tried to stand but Pancake held him where he was with one hand. Pancake smirked and shook his head. Book and Mase watched Delmar playing with the brown girl like a toy.

Delmar slid the pistol down the side of Wendy's face, tracing her jawline. Wendy twisted and tried to move away from Delmar and his pistol. Delmar grabbed Wendy by her hair and grinned.

"Don't move unless you want me to stick this pistol where it shouldn't go," Delmar said, his voice a hiss.

Tears fell from Wendy's eyes. She wept and moaned against the sock gag. Delmar turned again to Jayson who seemed in physical pain. He fought the cords holding him in the chair. Pancake squeezed Jayson's shoulder to keep him in place.

Mase and Book had moved just a few feet from Delmar. They stood silent, watching.

Delmar let the barrel of his gun follow the line of Wendy's shoulder. He looked down and leered at her barely hidden breasts under the see-through lacey fabric. Delmar turned again and looked at Jayson and smiled playfully.

"You better stop me before I do something you going to regret," Delmar said, looking at Jayson with contempt.

Delmar, evil as sin, allowed the pistol to play in the dip of Wendy's chest above her breasts. He followed the line of fabric of the cut of the negligee, pausing at the knotting which if untied would expose Wendy's breasts to all in the room.

The smiling Delmar looked down and paused admiring Wendy's figure. He smirked. He placed a hand on her knee. Wendy recoiled, but there was nowhere to go.

"I like a bitch that keeps herself up," Delmar said to Wendy. "See, you ain't no bush bitch all hairy and whatnot. That shit is a turn off for the kid. I mean, bitch shave your legs. Shave your arm pits. You ain't in the fucking jungle." Delmar said, looking at Wendy and then to Pancake and finally to Jayson. "Now, this bitch here, I could press up on. She care for herself. Bet she trimmed and keeping that shit nice and ready for the right pipe."

While Delmar spoke, Wendy cried. The cruel and callous man with the gun didn't seem to care. He let the pistol barrel find Wendy's left breast. With the touch of the barrel Wendy's gag muffled her outcry.

Delmar smirked. He turned and studied Jayson.

"You want me to stick this pistol where it shouldn't go?" Delmar asked with a smile. "Or should I give her my pipe? Or Pancake's?" He looked directly at Jayson. Behind him, Wendy was a blubbering mess.

"You ready to answer my questions?"

Jayson nodded his head. Jayson nodded and nodded. He tried to talk but the sock gag made it impossible to understand.

Delmar grinned at Wendy. Delmar studied the girl for a long moment and found himself excited being so close to her trembling form. He winked.

"Maybe," Delmar said, with a smile. "If things don't work out..." He trailed off. He shook off the thought and turned to Jayson.

"Okay, Jayson, I ain't got time for games. If you don't answer my questions, I'm going to make you regret ever seeing me," Delmar said, suddenly serious. "Where's my money?"

He removed the sock gag.

"Listen all the money I got is what you got," Jayson said.

Delmar grinned cruelly. He stuck out his lower lip and considered what Jayson said.

"You know Jayson, I've been on the streets since I was thirteen or fourteen. I been shot, stabbed, hit by a car, and nearly set on fire. I have dealt with rich and poor and liars and thieves. In the time I have been bouncing around I have had to make snap decisions about people. I had to decide if I could trust them or not in seconds." Delmar paused. "On the street trust is a big deal. We don't trust everyone. Trust is worth more than anything on the street. So, I have this trust radar. It's sort of a bullshit detector at the same time." Delmar had his pistol resting on his thigh as he talked. "I have learned how to tell if someone is lying. I'm pretty good."

"I'm not lying," Jayson said, imploringly.

Delmar looked at Jayson and studied the man in front of him.

"Yeah, you ain't lying about that," Delmar said, with a nod.

"Where did you get that money?" Delmar asked.

Jayson did not respond.

"Okay, you going to make me fuck your girl in front of you?" Delmar asked with a small smile.

"No, no," Jayson said, his voice rising. "You ain't got to do that."

"You went out with your friends? Right?" Delmar asked.

Jayson nodded his head.

"Mase, come here," Delmar said, never taking his eyes off Jayson.

Mase stepped forward with the paper bucket.

Delmar grabbed the bucket of quarters and dropped them in front of Jayson.

"You were at Face Down? Right?" Delmar asked.

"Yeah," Jayson said.

"You get a ride there?" Delmar asked.

Jayson didn't speak.

"Listen, Jayson, I ain't got no beef with you. I get you saw your opportunity and you took it. That's cool. But shit changed. This is now just a simple business transaction," Delmar said. "I just want my money. You give it back and our transaction is over." He paused. "If you want to test me and need to see drama then I can be all sorts of drama." Delmar looked at Wendy like she was a meal.

Jayson looked from the smiling dark man in front of him to the giant of a man and to the two boys standing behind them. Behind them sat Wendy shaken and crying.

"How in the fuck did you come up on my money?" Delmar asked.

Jayson retold the story of getting a job at the Imagination Station. His friends, Keyon and Gee inviting him out for dinner. They ended up at Face Down. They drank and it rained. They ran to the car. Gee found the bundle. They went to Key's condo and split the money. Gee had driven Jayson home and headed home afterward.

"So, this nigguh Gee is behind this?" Delmar asked.

"No, it wasn't like that," Jayson said. "He just said it was sitting there by the car when he climbed in."

"What that muthafucka do?" Delmar asked.

"He's a schoolteacher," Jayson said.

"Schoolteacher?" Delmar asked, skeptically.

"Yeah," Jayson said.

Delmar pouted, thinking. Something didn't add up.

"Okay, so the way I see it you and this Keyon and some teacher got my money. That right?" Delmar asked, unbelieving.

Jayson nodded his head.

Delmar looked around the apartment for Jayson's phone. He found it. He unlocked it and went to contacts. He searched for Keyon and Gee's phone numbers and addresses.

"Okay, I believe you," Delmar said. He shoved the sock back in Jayson's mouth. He looked to Pancake. "We taking this nigguh with us. He can get us the rest of the money."

Pancake smirked. He lifted Jayson up and waited for Delmar's instruction.

"I was thinking of capping you, but I was told to get all the money," Delmar said turning on the TV. "Bitch sit quiet and this shit should be over before your favorite TV show comes on."

He walked toward the front of the apartment and out the front door. Pancake followed with Jayson in his boxer shorts and Mase and Book following.

Chapter 27.
Four o'clock.

Delmar was driving. Mase was in the front passenger seat. Pancake was in rear of the car with Jayson between him and Book. The car moved as if on rails through the early morning. There was little to no traffic that early in the morning.

"So, Jayson, tell me about your new job," Delmar said as the Mercedes headed leisurely to the Palmer Wood.

"What?" Jayson asked.

"You got a new job? Right? Your friends took you out to celebrate? Right?" Delmar asked.

"Yeah," Jayson said dressed in boxer shorts from the middle of the back seat, next to the giant and the little boy. "I— I got a job at the MGM Grand."

"Are you making movies?" Delmar asked.

"What? No. Maybe," Jayson said, confused how the man who broke into his apartment just a few minutes before and threatened to rape Wendy was now trying to have a conversation like they were buddies. Jayson felt like he was experiencing whiplash with this suddenly cordial killer.

"I think that I might have seen one or two MGM films, but they ain't for me," Delmar said as the Mercedes drove toward Palmer Park.

"I liked the James Bond movies," said Mase.

"You would, little nigguh," Delmar said with a laugh.

"What about Wizard of Oz?" Pancake said.

"That was them?" Delmar asked.

"Yep," Pancake said with a growl.

"I don't know about that old white movie shit. I ain't seen a good white movie in forever. I liked that real deal shit like Boyz N the Hood, Menace II Society, and Judas and the Black Mesiah," Delmar said, turning the Mercedes SUV onto a quiet street.

The Mercedes Benz edged up to Key's condo.

"How we get in there?" Pancake asked.

"I don't know," Delmar said. "Let me think this one over."

Mase looked at the beaten-up man in the boxers and Pancake sitting in the backseat as calm as if this was a Sunday drive through the park. Mase tried to think about all he and Book had participated in since driving from Amicci's with Delmar and Pancake.

Delmar had threatened and then beaten up a boy and pistol whipped a girl and nearly killed the black cowboy. Pancake had punched and knocked out at least three people before they got to the bar. At the bar, the chaos was only taken to another level. For the first time that night or early morning Delmar floated the idea of raping and killing someone. Of course, Mase knew, being around Delmar the possibility of someone dying was always extremely high.

If they made it through the night or morning without someone dying Mase would be surprised. This was a crazy train to wherever it was headed, he and Book were on it until the end, unfortunately.

"Hey, Jayson," Delmar said, after a few minutes of thought. "This guy is your friend? Right?"

"Yep," Jayson said.

"You guys close?" Delmar asked, with a smile.

"Yep," Jayson said, suddenly uncertain.

"If you call him and tell him that if he doesn't give me back the money you and he stole from me I am going to kill you and your bitch, do you think he'll believe you?" Delmar asked, still smiling.

Jayson did not answer.

Delmar did not need an answer. He smiled evilly.

"Okay, let me make this clear so you understand what's at stake. I ain't play acting. I'm deadly serious. You three fucks have my money. I want it back. If you need to be motivated, I will go back to that bitch of yours and blow her head off for the loot." Delmar paused, letting what he said sink in. "Get me my money and you and your friends don't have to see us again. Fuck up and all shit goes tits up for you and your bitch and your friends."

Delmar studied Jayson. He handed him his cellphone which was already ringing. Pancake secured Jayson in the backseat. Book sat uncomfortably close to the man in his boxers.

"Jayson? What's up? I just was about to catch some sleep when you called. Everything all right?"

"No, it's not," Jayson said. "I need your help, Keyon."

"What's up?" Keyon asked.

Delmar smiled and gave a smug look.

"Well, you know the money we split?" Jayson asked.

"Yeah," Keyon said, slowly.

"Well, the guys that lost it want it back or they're going to kill me," Jayson said.

Delmar smirked in the front seat of the Mercedes.

"What?" Keyon asked, his voice suddenly tense.

"Yeah, I think that woman at Face Down gave them my address and one thing led to another."

Jayson blinked. Blood was in the corner of his mouth from where Pancake had hit him.

"What you going to do?" Keyon asked.

"What you mean?" Jayson asked.

There was silence.

"Key?" Jayson breathed.

"I mean, what *you* going to do?" Keyon asked.

"Key, I ain't playing," Jayson said, sounding frantic.

"I believe that, but why you calling me?" Keyon asked.

"You're involved," Jayson said, almost screaming.

"Am I? I mean, ain't no way they put two and two together and trace it back to me. Right?" Keyon asked.

Jayson was silent on the phone.

"Jayson, tell me you didn't give them my information," Keyon said.

"They were going to kill me and Wendy," Jayson said. "You heard me? Right?" Jayson was grasping at straws, nervously. "They still might."

Delmar gave a smug look.

"Man, what did you do?" Keyon asked.

"Key, come outside. I'm outside," Jayson said.

There was silence on the other end of the phone.

"Key, I ain't playing. They want their money. This is life or death," Jayson said. "It ain't like it was our money in the first place. Giving them back the money makes this all go away and makes sure we keep living."

"You outside?" Keyon asked, suddenly awake and alert.

"Yeah," Jayson said, softly.

"Why did you bring them to my place?" Keyon asked.

"They got my phone. They know it was you and Gee with me at Face Down," Jayson said, with a shake of his head.

"Fuck," Keyon said. "Fuck, fuck, fuck," he continued to say.

Delmar grinned at the torment he was putting the person through on the other end of the phone.

"Okay, I'll be down in five. I got to put on some clothes," Keyon said. "Fuck, Jay. Fuck, you fucked this all up."

"Thanks man," Jayson said but he wasn't sure Keyon even heard him.

Keyon kept saying "Fuck" for another ten seconds before the phone went silent.

"I like this guy," Delmar said with a broad smile. "He knows when shit is deep."

Mase looked at his hands. Book didn't say anything.

Delmar looked back at Jayson sitting between Pancake and Book.

"How you hook up with someone like that?" Delmar asked with a shake of his head.

"We grew up together," Jayson said.

Chapter 28.
Nearly five o'clock

Keyon was always the outlier, the oddball in the group. There was Gerald, the smart one. There was Jayson, the creative one. Then there was Keyon. He was always trying to think ahead and plan for the future. He had gone into the Army because he wanted to be all he could be. Three years in and he was already sure he was all he could be.

He was not a robot. He liked the discipline, but he did not like the lack of accountability of some in the ranks. The Army was not the elite of the nation but the average of the nation. The racism was thick and heavy in the ranks.

For the longest Keyon thought the men, he trained with, were going to shoot each other. They were the stupidest motherfuckers he had ever been forced to sleep with. Perhaps what made them stupid was that they thought because they were armed, they were untouchable.

Too often, while Keyon was in the ranks, white boys barked at black soldiers thinking that they were back in the 1800s. That barking always had a consequence. Always.

When his tour was over in Afghanistan he opted out.

Being a career soldier was not something Keyon wanted to consider. It was not a career for a black man, at least, not someone like Keyon.

He returned to the states and stumbled into his job at Up in Smoke. He had not planned it. It just happened.

That was the way he lived. There were no plans. He had learned in Afghanistan there was no point in planning. In an instance, plans changed. As a soldier he was trained to think on his feet and be strategic.

It was always Keyon first. Keyon take that. Keyon get that.

So, when Jayson had called that Friday morning and told him his predicament Keyon had thought to just hang up the phone. That was his first thought.

Jayson had fucked up. He had lost his share. It wasn't Key's problem.

Then, the longer he sat on the phone listening, the more Keyon found himself twisted with emotions. He wasn't supposed to care about Jayson losing his money or the threat of him dying if the unknown thugs didn't get their money. But it was Jayson.

Keyon climbed out of bed, dressed in his T-shirt and boxers. He searched his bedroom for clothes to put on as he thought of his next steps. He slipped on his jeans. He had his phone in his hand and instantly texted Gerald, the smart one. It was nearly five o'clock in the morning. He wasn't sure what Gerald would say in response to his text message, but as Keyon pulled on his jeans and slipped on a shirt he looked to his closet.

In the closet, in the floor safe, Keyon removed one of his pistols. He checked the clip and took a breath. He grabbed his black leather motorcycle jacket with the embroidered dragon wrapping around the back and stepped out dressed and ready for whatever might come.

Under his jacket Keyon had holstered one of his three pistols. On his hip was the other pistol. In his hand and then placed in the motorcycle jacket pocket was the third pistol. Whatever he was about to face he was going to face armed and ready for bear.

Keyon stopped at the table and scooped up the money which Gerald and Jayson had divided with him. He slipped the bills in the third plastic bag he had decided not to use earlier. Keyon slipped the plastic bag in the inside pocket of the motorcycle jacket and closed his eyes for just a second.

He stepped out of his condominium and looked left and right down the hall. It was still early on Friday the Thirteenth, Keyon realized. There was no one up or at least no one in the hall that early. Most people, normal people were sleeping, Keyon thought as he let his door close behind him.

"Fuck," Keyon said, annoyed he cared about Jay and Wendy and Gee and Gabi. "Fuck. Fuck. Fuck," Keyon said as he willed himself to march to the elevator and then push the down button.

Was he going to climb into the elevator in his high-priced Albert Kahn historic condominium and descend to his death? Was he ready to give up all he had acquired for Jay?

The elevator door opened. Keyon looked and peeked inside to see no one inside. The elevator door slowly closed.

Keyon looked down the hall not expecting to see anyone and what caught his eye was the stairway sign. It was only a hundred feet from the elevator. Keyon decided to use the stairs. It gave him time to think as he descended the four flights of stairs to the lobby.

In three flights he had created three scenarios and scrapped them all. One flight from the lobby Keyon considered another scenario.

He opened the locked stairway door and peeked out into the lighted lobby. There was no way to walk across the lobby without being seen. Then Keyon remembered he could have taken the elevator to the parking lot, just below the lobby. He ran back up the stairs to the second floor and pushed the elevator button and waited for the elevator to arrive.

While he waited, he checked his phone. It was now twenty minutes until five o'clock in the morning. Still no word from Gerald.

The elevator door opened, and Keyon climbed in and pressed the button for the parking garage.

The parking garage was just one floor lower than the lobby and held thirty cars at the lowest level. On the ramp to the street level was more parking for another thirty cars. Keyon walked past the Hyundai Elantra which was occupying his parking space instead of the Maserati Ghibli that had been stolen a few days ago. Seeing the Hyundai in his parking space angered Keyon all the more as he made his way to the street.

Without much thought Keyon had his pistol he had pocketed in his hand as he stepped onto the sidewalk looking for Jayson and the thugs threatening to kill him. He scanned the cars in front of the condominium and at that hour there was no one in the dozen cars parked on the street. Keyon looked back behind him and down the street and saw nothing which indicated Jayson or thugs.

"Damn," Keyon said, thinking he was going to have to cross the street and give his position away. He paused in the dark, looking for any movement and texted Jayson.

Where are you?

Walk 2 the corner. U'll see us.

Keyon hesitated. He knew whoever had Jayson's phone was not Jayson. He looked back and knew he was near one corner and the thugs had to be at the other corner. Just his luck.

"Fuck," Keyon said through gritted teeth.

Keyon looked down the quiet street and seeing nothing stepped out of the semidarkness and into the street. He quickly crossed the street and tried to allow the shapes of the street to hide him.

As he slipped between two cars Keyon had noticed a high-profile vehicle with two people at the corner. The SUV was parked with its nose sticking out and into the intersection.

"Fuck. Fuck. Fuck," Keyon said, closing his eyes and hearing his heartbeat in his ears as he walked forward toward the SUV. He looked down at his pistol in his hand and snapped off the safety and prepared for war.

Keyon moved forward, waiting for the first move of the SUV. The passenger door behind the driver opened as Keyon walked forward. Out of the SUV emerged a man who looked like a WWE wrestler dressed in a sweatsuit. The man was big. He looked like he should be playing football or, the idea of WWE wrestling came back to mind. He was one of those oversized humans that were shocking in city settings. He was supposed to be on an island or in the back woods or being discovered by archeologists somewhere, not in Detroit, Keyon thought as the mammoth of a man moved easily toward him.

At the same time, the driver's side window slid down and a deep brown smiling man with a pistol leaned out of the car window and looked at Keyon.

"You must be Key," the stranger said with a sickly-sweet smile.

Keyon looked at the two men. Keyon took a deep breath and lifted his right arm and leveled his gun at the driver. The driver seeing Keyon with a gun fired once, then twice and then again. Keyon felt a bullet whiz by his head. He braced his right arm with his left hand and pulled the trigger three times.

Six times the sound of fire and lead thundered on the quiet street. Keyon instinctively ducked after his third shot and watched the driver disappear from the car window.

Keyon blinked and tried to focus as the SUV, suddenly without a driver, crawled across the street under its own control. The Mercedes crashed into two cars across the street and stopped there with the engine running. The SUV instantly blocked the street in both directions.

At the same time, the giant, who had exited the SUV, moved quicker than Keyon imagined a man of his size should. Keyon turned to the black giant in the sweatsuit and realized his left arm was useless. He tried to lift it, but it hung limp against his side for some reason. He wanted to figure out what happened, but he did not have time to investigate.

Keyon focused and leveled his pistol in the direction of the locomotive of a man picking up speed and reaching out to grab him. Keyon pulled the trigger of his pistol three more times at the rushing mountain of a man. The three shots should have dropped the giant, but he kept coming. Keyon could not believe the giant took the three bullets and still did not stop or fall or slow down.

He gripped and regripped the pistol and pulled the trigger again. He got a chance to fire two more times before the monstrous man reached him. The block of obsidian bulled into Keyon and the force of the black train of a man bounced Keyon off a car and he and the giant ricocheted off the car and back onto the sidewalk. For a moment Keyon blacked out.

Keyon opened his eyes and found himself under the bulk of the man that was disproportionately bigger than anyone Keyon had ever met. Keyon rocked and tried to push the dead giant from atop him. Keyon twisted and wiggled his way from under the weight of the unmoving thug. He did a reverse sit up and got just enough leverage to push the dead man off him.

He was trying to get to his feet when he saw two more figures exit the crashed SUV.

"Damn," Keyon said, realizing he had no control of his left arm. It hung there limp and useless.

Keyon lifted his pistol and moved boldly forward. He knew he had been shot. He also knew he was pumping all sorts of adrenalin at the moment and as soon as the pain suppression supply stopped, he would feel the excruciating pain, but right now he was in fight mode.

He slowed a few yards from the SUV and looked for another attack.

"Jay, you alive?" Keyon asked angling his way to the SUV.

There was no answer from the SUV.

"Fuck," Keyon said. If he had any sense, he would turn around and call someone at Up in Smoke and get an all-cash doctor to patch him up, rather than playing like he was Rambo or Super fucking Vigilante.

Keyon crouched and crab walked the last few yards to the SUV.

In the dark he thought he saw two figures behind the SUV, lurking.

Keyon stopped. He was trembling. He was shot. He was trying to make sure he had enough ammunition to keep up the fight Jayson had brought to his front door.

He had fired his pistol three times, then three more times. Half dozen shots. Then two more times. That meant he had fired just eight times. He had another seven shots before he was empty on that pistol.

"Okay, muthafuckas, you want some more of me?" Keyon asked, crouched and ready for bear.

Keyon stood up and took a few more steps to the SUV. He looked into the driver's window and saw the man lying on the floor of the interior bleeding but unmoving.In the backseat was a slumped over Jayson dressed in his boxers.

Keyon walked to the back of the SUV. The two figures were gone. He made sure they weren't hiding and waiting for the chance to blow his head off.

He returned to the SUV and checked the driver. He was dead. He was also carrying the plastic bundle that Jayson had been carrying earlier. Keyon slipped the money into his jacket and then went to attend to Jayson.

Jayson was wrecked. He had been beaten up. He was fucked up but breathing, as best as Keyon could tell he was just beaten up and not shot.

Keyon removed the sock gag and dragged his friend from the SUV awkwardly with one hand.

Jayson came to enough to walk, and he and Keyon walked away from the SUV and to the front of the condo.

"Come on," Keyon said and dragged Jayson to the parking garage.

Keyon chirped the alarm on the Hyundai and deposited Jayson in the passenger seat. He climbed under the steering wheel and made a call to Up in Smoke feeling the pain gripping at his left shoulder.

"Brittany, this is Keyon, I need you to call Cedric and tell him I need a little help, off the books," Keyon said as he started the car. "Tell him to meet me at his office in twenty. If he's there before me he can have a bonus." Keyon rang off. His left arm was bleeding pretty bad, but he could not tell exactly where he had been shot. He had to get to Cedric's office before he went into shock or passed out from blood loss. The drive was only going to take about fifteen minutes if that.

"Jay, you with me?" Keyon asked.

Jayson looked like he had been through a meat grinder. He was all sorts of beaten. His face was a lumpy mess. His nose was caked with blood and if Keyon had to guess it was probably broken.

Jayson opened an eye and spoke. "I'm with you," he said. He closed his eye and fell silent.

Keyon backed the Hyundai out of the parking space and headed toward the street. He turned right and headed toward the main street a few blocks away.

"Fuck," Keyon said as he drove toward downtown. Cedric's office was not that far away, but Keyon had to be careful as he drove that Friday morning. He was shot. Jayson, in Keyon's medical evaluation, was all sorts of fucked. All he needed was the police to get involved.

*　　*　　*

Mase and Book ran from the SUV. The pair ran from Trumbull and toward Hubbard Richard. They ran. They had run into trouble and out of trouble and now they were uncertain where they were running.

At the first main street Mase stopped Book and the two boys looked at each other, shaken.

"Pancake dead," Book said, shocked by the words he uttered.

Mase nodded his head.

"Del too," Mase said and saying it made it real.

Book and Mase were headed away from all the shooting and the crashed Mercedes.

Someone was screaming behind them, but neither looked back. They just kept running.

"What are we going to do?" Book asked.

"Ain't much we can do," Mase said. He took a breath. "Suppose we head back to Chocolate and tell him what happened."

Book smirked. He looked at Mase uncertain.

"He ain't going to be happy," Book said.

Mase nodded.

"It ain't our fault," Mase said.

Book nodded his head. He looked at Mase unsure.

"It ain't our fault," Mase said again. "We did everything we were supposed to do."

Book nodded his head.

"We just kids. We ain't gangstas. We didn't even have burners," Mase said, trying to convince himself.

"If we had burners, do you think you would have shot back?"

"Hell yeah. No hesi," Mase said, pulling Book along. They were on a street corner, trying to figure out the fastest way back to West

Downtown. "If I had a Glock or an AK, I would have to protect myself. No one else is."

Book nodded his head and smiled.

*   *   *

In the Hyundai Keyon drove feeling the pain starting to radiate through his left arm. Jayson was shirtless and wearing boxer shorts in the passenger seat beside him. Keyon smiled at how the pair must look that morning.

A little after five o'clock in the morning Keyon pulled up to a nondescript building in the Atkins Avenue Historic District. To most the building looked like a house, but Keyon knew it was the unofficial offices of Cedric Brewer, the unofficial medic for Up in Smoke.

Keyon pulled into the driveway and drove to the rear of the house and parked. Cedric was waiting with a big smile on his face. He was dressed in hospital scrubs, nitrile gloves and a surgical mask when Keyon opened his driver's side door.

"I was promised a bonus if I beat you here," Cedric said with a chuckle from behind his surgical mask.

"Yeah, yeah," Keyon said. "I'm leaking Ced and don't know how long I got to explain shit. Need you to take care of me and my partner. On the low. I'm good for the cash. You know," Keyon was saying, his hand on the front of the Hyundai and suddenly he was rushing toward the driveway, unconscious.

When Keyon opened his eyes, Jayson was the first person he recognized. Jayson was smiling, even though his face was swollen from being pummeled earlier. Keyon was lying on a bed and tried to sit up. The effort to sit up felt like he was bench pressing a thousand pounds. His left side felt stiff and painful. Keyon tried to sit up again and on the second attempt made it halfway to sitting up. He noticed his left arm was in a sling.

"You okay?" Jayson asked.

"Naw, nigguh. I was shot," Keyon said with a snicker.

"Yeah. I don't know what I was thinking," Jayson said, wearing a pair of gym shorts and a Motown Museum T-shirt.

"Why you dressed in that?" Keyon asked.

"It's all he had," Jayson said, with a shoulder shrug.

"Jay, look in my jacket," Keyon said. "There's something for you."

Jayson went to the leather jacket, searched the jacket, and found the two Ziploc bags of money.

"What the fuck?" Jayson asked, shocked.

"Yeah, I mean I took a bullet for you. You know we can't come out losing," Keyon said.

"Damn," Jayson said.

"Ced, get me some scrubs. We can't stay here," Keyon said.

"What? He got scrubs?" Jayson asked.

"Yeah, he's fucking with you. He has to have an extra pairs of scrubs. We'll get you squared away," Keyon said, adjusting his focus and trying to take in the room where he and Jayson were waiting. "Okay, you know you only get one bag."

Jayson smiled.

In walked Cedric still dressed in his scrubs, no nitrile gloves or surgical mask. He was a dark man with thick eyebrows, dark eyes, a straight but broad nose and small toothed smile. He had small shoulders, a bit of a potbelly and short legs. On his feet were Crocs.

"Ced? We good? You do your magic?" Keyon asked.

"I did," Cedric said, his voice had a southern twang to it.

"How's my boy?" Keyon asked.

"He's much better than you," Cedric said with a serious tone.

"I'll be fine. How much I owe you?" Keyon asked swinging his legs out of bed and wincing with the effort.

"You are going to be in pain for a few days. I got some Vicodin if you want it," Cedric said.

"No, I think I'll be fine," Keyon said, climbing out of bed still dressed in his jeans. He scanned the small room for his jacket. It was resting on a small table with his two other guns.

Cedric walked up to Keyon and looked at the guns and then Keyon.

"Should I be worried?" Cedric, the street doctor asked.

"About what?" Keyon asked, with a chuckle. "It was just another Thursday night in Detroit."

Keyon peeled off twenty bills and handed them to Cedric.

Jayson and Keyon exited Cedric's home/office and found themselves back in the rear of the house.

"I wiped down the car as best I could," Cedric said. "You might want to get it detailed. Nothing gets the attention of people more than lots of blood in a car."

"Yeah, Ced," Keyon said, climbing into the car gingerly.

"You want me to drive?" Jayson asked.

"Naw, I'm fine," Keyon said.

Keyon started the car and as he backed the car out of the driveway his phone rang. Keyon looked at the caller ID and smirked.

He tapped the phone and the call connected to the Bluetooth of the car.

"What's up Key?" Gerald said.

"Shit," Keyon said to Gerald.

"Gee? Where are you?" Asked Jayson.

"I'm at home. I'm getting ready to head to work," Gerald said. "Jay? What are you doing with Key this early?"

"It's a long story. We just leaving--" Jayson began only to stop himself.

"We just leaving from over a friend of mines," Keyon said, interrupting Jayson. He shook his head at Jayson. "Was trying to check on you to make sure you got home safely."

"Yeah, I got home about one and you know Gabi was not happy," Gerald said.

"I bet," Keyon smiled, backing onto Atkinson, and heading back toward Jayson's home. "Well, just wanted to make sure you were good."

"I'm good," Gerald said.

"Okay, teach, have a good day. Catch up with your boys this weekend?" Keyon asked.

"For sure," Gerald said.

"All right. Holler," Keyon said.

"What was that all about?" Jayson asked, confused.

"The teach don't need to worry about shit that don't concern him. You know that," Keyon said.

"Yeah, I suppose you're right."

Keyon and Jayson drove into the morning and back toward Jayson's house that Friday morning after a memorable Thursday night in Detroit.

www.ingramcontent.com/pod-product-compliance
Lightning Source LLC
Chambersburg PA
CBHW010729310726
48971CB00009B/2778